PATTY DUKE

and MYSTERY MANSION

Authorized Edition featuring the
characters created by Sidney Sheldon
for the well-known television series
THE PATTY DUKE SHOW

by Doris Schroeder

illustrated by
Wilbur A. Howe

WHITMAN PUBLISHING COMPANY • Racine, Wis.

Contents

1   *Who's Who?*

A bright summer morning on Brooklyn Heights. A sliver of breeze off the busy East River setting the leaves dancing greenly along the quiet streets. A cocky little tugboat pulling its string of barges and giving out impudent hoots at the giant liner on its way out to sea. And in the Lanes' two-story brick home above the Promenade, a stir of awakening.

Patty Lane opened one eye to look at the tiny alarm clock beside her bed. She was startled to see that its hands indicated seven. She should have been up half an hour ago! She would be late for school—again!

She started to sit up and then sank back with a blissful smile. School was out for the summer. There was no reason to dash around madly. She could snatch another half hour.

She was just drifting off again when a stir in

9

the other twin bed brought her wide-awake once more. Cathy! Cathy was here—right in this very room with her! Cathy—the cousin she had been hearing about all her life, it seemed. Cathy— whose father and her own were brothers, identical twin brothers. Cathy had finally come to America to live. Cathy who looked exactly—but that was the part she still could hardly believe! She bounced out of bed and tiptoed over·for a hasty look at her sleeping cousin.

Being Patty, who always acted on impulse and hardly ever looked where she was going, she stumbled over Cathy's neatly lined-up slippers and bumped against the bed.

The honey blond head on the pillow turned abruptly. The face, with its wide eyes that stared in bewilderment for a moment before they warmed into recognition, was so like Patty's own that it brought a startled whisper from her. "Cuckoo!"

Cathy sat up smiling. "Like staring into a look- ing glass, isn't it?" she said. "It gives me a strange feeling, too."

"Let's look in the mirror!" Patty suggested quickly, and Cathy slipped out of bed to hurry over and stand beside her cousin before the tall pier glass that reflected them from head to foot.

Except for a slight difference in height, resulting from Cathy's more erect bearing and Patty's careless slouch, they looked exactly alike. They stared at their reflections wonderingly a moment, then Patty wrinkled her nose and made a funny face. Cathy copied her expression exactly and both of them broke into gales of laughter.

"Stupendous!" Patty gurgled when she had simmered down a bit. "I bet we could have a ball fooling people!"

"I suppose we could, at that," Cathy agreed.

"We'll think up a gag," Patty told her confidently. "I'm good at that." Then she added honestly, "Only sometimes it doesn't work out just right, and I fall on my face!"

"As my dad would say," Cathy said reassuringly, " 'too much success could become a bore.' He usually says it after he's made a horrible score at golf!"

Patty grinned. "He makes sense." Then she said, a little apologetically, "If you don't mind my saying it, Cath, you don't talk as funny as I expected. I thought you'd be saying things like 'It's a braw bricht moonlicht nicht' and such."

"Dad and I were in Scotland hardly long enough for that," Cathy explained with a smile. "He was sent to Edinburgh by the newspaper syndicate he writes for now—to cover a special situation. We didn't get about the countryside very much."

"Oh, is it just the people in the little places that talk like that? I'm so disappointed. I thought they all did!"

"Lots of them do. And almost everyone has the Scottish burr—you know, the way they say their r's—br-rrr!"

"Sounds as if you were shivering with cold!" Patty said with a giggle. "Maybe that's how it started. Is it cold there?"

"Just brisk," Cathy told her, and then went on, her eyes taking a faraway look of remembering. "Dad and I loved it. We used to walk out into a little park beside the water when my work was finished each afternoon—"

"You *worked?* Doing what?"

"I was Dad's amanuensis," Cathy explained.

"His which?" The word was a stranger.

"His secret'ry," Cathy translated hastily.

"Oh! Hey, I like that word. You'll have to teach it to me so I can spring it on the kids when they come to meet you. It'll knock them on their ears!"

Cathy laughed. "That will be something to write Dad about. I don't think he's up on that bit of slang."

"What did you do as a secretary?" Patty didn't dare try the new word yet.

"Dad let me do all his correspondence and type his reports. He said I was the best amanu—I mean, secret'ry—he'd ever had. In his reports from Paris—"

Patty interrupted excitedly. *"Paris?* Have you actually been to Paris?"

Cathy answered calmly. She couldn't help enjoying the surprise and admiration of her cousin.

"Oh, yes. And we were in Berlin—West Berlin, of course—and London. I liked London. We never missed a performance of the Royal Ballet last season."

"Ooh!" Patty was really dazzled. For once she was speechless.

Cathy glanced out the window and her gaze fixed suddenly on something across the silvery river. "Patty! Look!"

Patty dashed to the window and stared out to see what had caught Cathy's eye. "What is it?"

"Is that actually—I mean to say—" Cathy pointed, unable to say more in her excitement.

"It's only the Statue of Liberty." Patty waved it off. "Gosh! I thought a ship was burning up or something."

"*Only* the Statue of Liberty!" Cathy echoed. "Patty, ever since I can remember, Dad has talked about sailing past that statue with me some day and settling down to live in our own country after bouncing all around the world for so long."

"But think of all the places you've been and the things you've seen!"

"Anyone can get tired of traveling. Dad would have preferred to come here, this time, but he had to go to Africa. It always happens when we make plans to come home for good." Cathy sighed. "Poor Dad."

"Wouldn't you have liked to go to Africa with him?" Patty asked.

Cathy shook her head. "Dad thought, and I agreed, that it would be better for me to come home to meet my family. Things are rather unsettled down there and he may be dashing about all over the continent." Her eyes were troubled.

Patty saw it, and she gave her sober-faced cousin a quick hug. "Well, we're simply delighted to have you here, and we're glad you decided to come. And won't we have fun looking alike! We'll get our clothes just alike for school and play jokes on the teachers. And—" She broke off abruptly, glancing toward the hall door.

Cathy was surprised to see her put her finger to her lips for silence and then hastily tiptoe to the door and fling it open, exclaiming, "Ha! Caught in the act!"

But there was only an oversized shaggy white and black dog, with a waving plume of a tail, waiting to dash in. "Oh, it's only you, Tiger," she said crossly, sticking out her foot to hold him outside. "Scram!"

But Tiger was staring past her at Cathy, the identical copy of the girl at the door. He gave a scared whimper, tucked his tail between his legs, and turned to gallop away through the hall and galumph down the stairs.

Patty glared after him and then slammed the door. "Guess he thought he was seeing double," she said grimly.

"Whom did you expect would be there?" asked Cathy.

"That snoopy little brother of mine!" Patty muttered. "He's always listening in on people."

"He seems a nice little chap," Cathy ventured calmly.

"He's a monster. He listens in on our extension phone, and I have to bribe him to stay off the line. He's a pest."

"I've heard that's a stage all boys go through,

as they grow up," Cathy said cheerfully. "He'll outgrow it."

"Not him," Patty said darkly. "He'll get worse." She brightened suddenly. "Hey, let's take him down a peg!"

"How?" Cathy was wary.

"Well, yesterday, you remember, he was saying that we needn't think we could ever fool him on which was which of us. Let's take him up on that!"

It was only a few minutes later that Natalie Lane was passing her daughter's room. She was about to go on and let the two cousins sleep awhile longer, when she heard a giggle inside. She tapped on the door. "Girls, are you up?"

"Oh, yes, Aunt Natalie!" came Cathy's well-modulated voice.

And Patty's voice answered, "Bright-eyed and bushy-tailed, Mom!"

Natalie sighed. She hoped some of Patty's slanginess would disappear, now that Cathy was here to set an example. But, and she shuddered at the thought, it might work the other way!

"Don't be long, girls," she called. "I'll go down and start breakfast."

"I'll go with you, Aunt Natalie," Cathy answered, and a moment later, Cathy—or a reasonable facsimile garbed in Cathy's tweedy outfit of sweater and skirt—joined Natalie in the hall.

Natalie told her, "You look as if you had slept well your first night home in the States, dear."

Patty hesitated to answer. This would be the test. She swallowed hard and then, in an excellent imitation of Cathy's well-bred accents, she said, "Very well indeed, Aunt Natalie."

"I'm so glad, dear. I was afraid Patty would keep you awake half the night, asking questions about Scotland and all the other places where you've lived."

"Not at all," Patty said carefully. And as they went sedately down the stairs arm in arm, she could hardly keep from laughing and confessing the hoax. But she held it back. The real test was still to come.

Patty was a little jittery as she greeted "Uncle

Martin" and "Cousin Ross" a few minutes later when they sauntered into the kitchen. Natalie was busy explaining the electrical gadgets to "Cathy" as they prepared breakfast.

"Where's my lazy daughter?" Martin asked. "Has she managed to slough off her labors on you already?"

Patty almost gave the show away by defending herself, but she managed to hold her tongue in time.

"Stop fussing, dear. Cathy and I are having a good time," Natalie told him. "Patty's coming down directly. You know how she dawdles over her hairdo."

"Why can't she do it some simple way, neat like Cathy's here? It would look one hundred per-cent better. Most of the time I'd swear it looks as if she had combed it with an egg beater!"

Patty gulped and reached hastily for the sugar bowl in front of Ross and loaded it on the tray to carry into the dining room. Her face was notice-ably pinker.

As she disappeared through the swinging door,

Martin asked Ross, "Why are you staring after Cathy, Ross?"

"No reason," Ross said, staring innocently at his father. "Just lookin'." And he followed "Cathy," whistling. Off key, as usual, though he always hotly denied it.

"We won't wait for the late Miss Lane," Martin said sternly. "And nothing is to be kept warm for her."

"Hey, I know why Patty's hair looks like a bird's nest," Ross said as they sat down in the dining room. "It's because she's such a birdbrain. Ha!"

"That's enough, Ross. Eat your breakfast," his mother said severely.

But Ross had turned to Patty. "Don't let ol' Patty butter you up, Cathy. Before you know it, she'll be wearing everything you own and actin' like it belonged to her!"

"Ross!" Martin rattled his paper at the boy.

"Somebody's gotta warn her what a pill she's roomin' with!" Ross insisted. He turned to red-faced Patty. "You'll find out if you try to borrow something that belongs to *her!*"

"One more word and you'll leave the room without your breakfast," his father thundered.

Natalie looked distressed. "I'm afraid our two are both spoiled just a little, Cathy. Ross is thoughtless and Patty *is* sometimes a bit too possessive about her things. But I'm sure she'll learn to share with you gladly."

"Oh, yeah!" Ross hooted, staring at Patty. "You won't catch that one letting go of anything once she gets her hot little hands on it."

"Cathy" abruptly pushed back her chair and jumped to her feet in tears. Before anyone could move to stop her, she had run out of the room.

2   *The Gift*

Martin Lane and his wife looked at each other in astonishment as the door slammed after tearful "Cathy."

But Ross laughed gleefully. "Got her that time!"

"Just what do you mean by that?" Martin demanded sternly.

"She didn't have *me* fooled for a minute," their ten-year-old boasted. "That wasn't Cathy. That was sneaky ol' Patty tryin' to fool us!"

"Ridiculous!" Martin stormed. "March right after Cathy this minute, young fellow, and whatever it was that made her cry, you'll apologize for."

"But it wasn't Cathy, Dad," Ross insisted. "I knew it when she reached for the sugar bowl and I saw that ID bracelet she was wearing. It's the one that Patty's new boyfriend, Richard, gave her last week when they started going steady."

"She must have loaned it to Cathy to wear," Natalie suggested quickly.

"Uh-uh," Ross shook his head. "Not her! I heard her tell Richard she'd never take it off, even in the shower, and then she let him kiss her as a pledge, and—"

"Finish your breakfast and go on over to Davey's house to listen to that shortwave program you wanted to hear," his father said firmly.

"Yes, sir," Ross agreed meekly. He gobbled down the remainder of his cereal, finished off his milk, and scooted out before his father could change his mind.

When the front door had closed, his parents looked at each other grimly. "I'm a bit uncertain what we said about Patty that could have upset her so." Martin frowned. "Do you remember?"

"Well, I did agree that she is a little selfish. Oh, dear! I'd better go talk to her." She started away reluctantly, as if dreading it.

"Wait," Martin said thoughtfully. "Let's talk over a plan of action first." He glanced at his watch. "But I can't spare too much time, or old J. R. will have a chance to get one of his inspirations to rewrite my editorial for the Saturday edition before I get there to defend my lofty opinions!"

"All right, Mr. Managing Editor. What can we do to convince her we didn't mean it?"

Upstairs, Patty was dramatically telling Cathy, "Now I know what my family really thinks about me! They despise me! They think I'm a perfect drip!"

"Oh, Patty! I'm sure they don't feel that way in the least. They adore you, really!"

"No, they don't." Patty sniffed, looking her most tragic. "I think I'll run away and be a circus performer. I can see myself, a lonely bareback rider, in spangles and one of those cute, fluffy skirts, on a white horse—" She was becoming interested in the picture.

Cathy bit her lip to keep back a grin as she listened, then interrupted innocently, "I thought you didn't like horses since you fell off one in the park when you were a little girl."

Patty was jolted out of her dream. "Yeah, that's right. They always try to bite me. I guess that's out. So maybe I'll enter a monastery and wear a long brown robe and sandals, and—"

"I'm afraid you wouldn't be very welcome there, either," Cathy giggled. "No women wanted."

"That's right," Patty sighed. "Well—"

A knock interrupted them. Natalie put her head in to remind them that breakfast was getting cold on the table.

"Better hurry down and tell Dad good-bye, Patty dear," she added lightly, "but, please, no more play-acting!" She gestured toward Patty's wrist. "Especially when you're wearing that precious new bracelet of yours!"

And as Patty's jaw dropped in astonishment, Natalie ducked out again and closed the door behind her.

Patty blinked after her a moment, and then a happy grin grew on her face. "Cathy! They knew all the time! They were just trying to break me down and make me confess I wasn't you. They were just teasing!"

"I felt it was something of the sort," Cathy assured her. She was surprised to see Patty scowl suddenly.

"But Ross certainly sounded as if he meant it," Patty said suspiciously.

"Never mind all that now," Cathy told her lightly, linking her arm with Patty's and drawing her toward the door. "If someone doesn't feed me pretty soon, I shall start gnawing on that Sheraton chair I see over there in the corner. And that should be costly to my dad as well as hard on my digestion!"

They had reached the lower hall and were hurrying toward the dining room when the front doorbell rang.

A uniformed messenger boy stood there with a small tissue-wrapped parcel in his hand. "Lane?" he asked Patty briskly as she opened the door. "Are you Miss—"

"Patty Lane, *in* person!" Patty reached for the small parcel.

The freckle-faced messenger held it away. "The name is *Cathy* Lane. And she's gotta sign for it."

Cathy hurried forward. "I'm Cathy Lane."

"Twins, huh?" The boy looked them over impudently as Cathy was signing. "Like wow!" He winked at Patty.

But Patty sniffed at him and closed the door hastily. "Who's it from, Cath?"

"My dad, I imagine. He's always surprising me with things," Cathy said happily. She was beginning to look puzzled as she turned the parcel over and over looking for some sign that she had guessed right. "That's queer," she said, "there's no writing or stamp on it."

"Open it!" Patty could hardly wait. "I'm dying!"

"What is going on here?" It was Martin on his way out. Natalie was close behind him, peering eagerly over his shoulder.

"It's a mystery package!" Patty told them excitedly. "Cathy just got it. Please open it, Cath!"

"Suppose you curb your rude curiosity and let

Cathy manage her own affairs," Martin told his daughter sternly. "Scoot!" He waved toward the dining room. "And if you're not hungry, start clearing the table. That should keep you busy."

"Oh, I don't mind opening it right here. I haven't the foggiest idea who sent it," Cathy said hastily and started to tear off the tissue wrappings. "Let's all see what it is."

The wrappings drifted to the floor, and a folded note fell unnoticed with them.

There was a velvet box inside. Cathy opened the old-fashioned hook clasp. She gasped as she saw the heavy gold-link necklace that lay on the satin lining, circling a heavy pendant set with four clear green stones.

"How lovely!" she said, lifting it out to show them.

Natalie touched it, her eyes wide with awe. "Why, I believe it's real. And these stones are emeralds, I'm sure. I thought at first it was costume jewelry."

Patty was too dazzled to speak for a moment, but when she found her tongue she told Cathy,

"You *must* know who'd give you a present like this! Did you meet some prince or duke or something on the plane? You *must* have!" Her eyes sparkled with excitement. "You're holding out on us!"

"Truly, I'm not," Cathy said seriously. "And actually, if I had met some Prince Charming, I'm afraid it wouldn't have been very romantic. It was such a bumpy trip that practically everyone but the crew was dreadfully ill and alarmed."

Patty was disappointed, but a moment later she noticed the folded note on the floor and swooped to recover it. "Ha!" She waved it at the others. "This must have fallen out." She flipped it open and managed to glance at the signature before her mother snatched it from her hand. "Owen Trevett! Was he a good-looker, Cath?"

Natalie glared at her daughter and then handed the note to Cathy apologetically. "Please don't bother to answer her, Cathy. She has forgotten her manners, I'm afraid."

"I told you to scoot, five minutes ago," Martin snapped at his daughter. "Or would you rather spend the day in your room?"

"Please, Uncle Martin, I want to tell Patty and all of you about Mr. Trevett. He wasn't a bit romantic. He's a perfectly adorable little old gentleman who was on the plane."

"But why did he send you this?" Patty asked, blunt as usual.

"I suppose he explains in his note, if you'll keep quiet and let your cousin read it," Natalie said reprovingly.

Cathy skimmed hastily through the note. "Mr. Trevett says he wants me to have the necklace because I was so kind—Oh, actually, Aunt Natalie, all I did was try to make him comfortable during the dreadful lightning storm we passed through over the Atlantic. The stewardesses had their hands full with the ladies and babies, and old Mr. Trevett seemed so miserable and frightened."

"The lightning storm must have been exciting!" Patty interjected a bit enviously.

"More gruesome than exciting," Cathy admitted, "especially for Mr. Trevett. He had never been aloft in a storm. His wife was afraid of flying, so they had never done much of it."

"I suppose she was terrified, too," Natalie said sympathetically.

"She wasn't with him. He lost her a couple of months ago, after they had traveled all over Europe for the past twenty years trying to find some place where she could recover from her illness, whatever it was. He hadn't intended to return to this country, but it seems some emergency had come up here and he had to make the trip. But he's planning to go back—to where she is now—as soon as his affairs are settled."

"Poor chap! All his money probably can't help him much in his loneliness," Martin said thoughtfully.

"Oh, you know him, Uncle Martin?" Cathy asked.

"I don't know *him,* but I know the Trevett mansion. It's that huge old place we pass as we walk to church, Nat," he told his wife.

"Oh, the one that's partly boarded up. It's perfectly fascinating! It must have forty rooms at least, and I'm sure it's well over a hundred years old. I'd adore having a good look around inside, but I've never been able to think up an excuse to get in past that grim old caretaker and his wife!" Natalie admitted sadly. "It must be full of antiques!"

"Why don't you come with me when I take this necklace back to Mr. Trevett? I can't accept it, really," Cathy said.

"Oh, no!" Patty wailed. "I was counting on borrowing it to wear to the senior prom with Richard next June!"

"I'm sorry, Patty," Cathy spoke soberly. "But this is far too valuable for me to take just for trying to help a frightened old gentleman forget his fears. And I'm sure Aunt Natalie agrees with me."

Natalie sighed. "I *have* to agree, Cathy, but I hate to see it go! It would look lovely with my new chiffon."

"Well,"—Patty was ready to settle for next best—"I think I'll go with you when you return it. I want to see what Spook Castle looks like inside, too!"

"What did you call it?" Martin asked with a frown.

"Spook Castle. Ross and Davey call it that. They got in somehow one day and roamed all over the place while the caretakers were out shopping or something. They claim they heard a ghost up in a big, dark old picture gallery on the top floor. I think they made that up, but I'm going to ask Mr. Trevett what we have to do to see the family ghost, if there is one!" Patty planned happily.

"Sorry to disappoint you, ladies, but I intend to take Cathy over to return that bauble myself, this evening. And there'll be no sight-seeing excursion from here on the program."

There were two disappointed faces and Patty wanted to argue, but her mother stopped her. "Dad is right, dear. After all, he is the head of the house and Cathy's legal guardian in this country." She sighed and turned to her husband with a little toss of her head. "But don't be too smug, Martin Lane! Because Patty and I will find a way to get an invitation someday!"

Martin laughed. Then after a glance at his watch, he dashed toward the door, retrieving hat and briefcase on the way. "See you later," he called back and disappeared down the steps.

Patty looked gloomy, but the phone rang just then and she hurried excitedly to answer it.

Cathy and Natalie looked again at the necklace, and Natalie held it up against her throat. Then she thrust it suddenly into Cathy's hands. "Here! Hide this before I go primitive and club you over the head and run off with it!"

They were both laughing when they heard Patty's voice. "Why, sure. Come on and bring the gang! Cathy wants to meet all of you. Right around two will be elegant. Bring your new records and we'll really have a wingding!"

Cathy looked surprised, but Natalie struck herself on the forehead and groaned. "I knew it! I broke a bridge date to take you two sight-seeing today, and now look!" Then she began to figure on her fingers, muttering, "Let's see, that means more soda pop, another gallon of ice cream, six packages of cookies,"—she wandered away down the hall still counting—"and two gallons of milk. . . ."

Patty's voice came from inside the study. "Hi, Babs! Drop over this afternoon. It's a blast. For my cousin. I'm calling everybody."

Cathy listened uneasily. At that moment she wished fervently that Patty weren't so eager to show her off. Patty's gang would be sure to expect her to be gay and uninhibited like Patty, because they looked so much alike. And she knew she couldn't possibly pretend to be that way, especially with a lot of strangers.

She had an unhappy feeling that they'd think she was—what was the word Patty used?— *snooting* them.

3   *The Blast*

While Patty chattered on the phone, Cathy took time to run upstairs again and stow the necklace safely in a dresser drawer. When she returned, Patty was still busy, so Cathy went on to the dining room.

Natalie was there, eating a hearty breakfast and checking over a grocery list. "Have some breakfast, dear," she said between bites and pencil scribbles. "It's keeping hot on the sideboard."

"Thanks, Aunt Natalie," Cathy said and proceeded to help herself.

"I suppose Patty is still occupying the study and tying up the phone," her mother said glumly. "I've tried three times to cut in, but the chatter was too thick."

Cathy nodded with a sigh. "Aunt Natalie, do you mind if I interrupt you?"

"Not at all. Is something wrong, dear?"

"Not really, except that I've been wondering if I won't seem dreadfully stupid to Patty's friends because I don't know anything about baseball and things like that. I don't even know who your American recording artists are."

Natalie laughed and waved it away. "Don't worry, dear. Five minutes after they get here, they'll have the record player going. And that will be the end of conversation. Everyone will be much more interested in the Mashed Potato and the Shag."

Cathy looked startled. "The which?"

"Just a couple of native dances of the Teener Tribe." Natalie shrugged. "You won't have any trouble learning them, I'm sure."

Cathy still seemed worried, but Patty came dashing in just then, looking annoyed. "Gosh," she said, "seems as if everybody's away to the country or down at the beach today."

"Fine!" Natalie started to tear up the grocery list. "Then I can forget this and we'll go sight-seeing!"

"Oh, I didn't mean *everybody* can't come. I

meant there's only going to be a couple—well, maybe ten or so."

Natalie made a wry face. "I knew it was too good to be true! And now if you'll just stay off the phone for five minutes, I'll order this stuff for your hungry horde."

But as Natalie started for the kitchen to use the extension phone there, it began to ring and Patty tried to make a dash. Natalie caught her by the sleeve. "Whoa! If that's one of your half-hour calls, your guests won't get anything to eat this afternoon. You know how Mr. Schwartz is about his deadline on phone orders."

"OK," Patty said, while the phone continued to ring in the kitchen, "but please tell 'em I'll call back in five minutes, whoever it is."

"I'll make it ten, and you eat some breakfast," her mother said sternly and hurried to the kitchen.

"Richard's coming," Patty announced to her cousin. She toyed with her bracelet. "And he has a new car!" She giggled. "Wait till the other kids see it. He says it's a humdinger."

"I'm afraid I don't know that make," Cathy

said regretfully. "We don't see them in Europe."

Patty burst into giggles as she explained that the humdinger wasn't any special make of car; it was just a keen one. "Richard's father promised to let Richard have a car if he got good marks all term. And he did." She giggled again. "Good thing his dad doesn't know it took the whole football squad to help him get by his Latin!"

Natalie came in briskly, crumpling the grocery list. "Well, I caught Mr. Schwartz just in time. I had to wheedle him a little, but we'll get our groceries."

"Who called, Mom?" Patty asked quickly.

"Oh, it was just Dad. He had quite a time fixing the date for himself and you, Cathy. Some bossy woman who answered his phone told Dad that Mr. Trevett wasn't seeing anyone because he was too tired. She said she was Mira Burton, Mr. Trevett's niece."

"Perhaps she knows best," Cathy said thoughtfully.

Natalie chuckled. "Mr. Trevett didn't think so. He came on the line, Dad says, and said he'd be most happy to see you and he wasn't the least bit tired and he hadn't told anybody to do his thinking for him. He was furious, and the poor woman finally hung up. Dad says she was so angry she sputtered."

"Hooray for Mr. Trevett!" Patty waved a salute. Then she saw Cathy was wearing a puzzled look. "What's wrong, Cath?"

"I was just thinking. I'm sure Mr. Trevett told me that he was the *last* of the Trevetts."

"Well, maybe she said 'nurse' and Dad thought it was 'niece'," Patty suggested quickly.

"That's probably the answer!" Natalie agreed. "You'll find out tonight just who she is, I'm sure, Cathy. Not that it's important, I'd say. The important thing is for you two to march yourselves down to the basement and start getting the play-room in order."

"But it is! There's just a few records lying around—and we'll be using them—" Patty pro-tested, but vainly.

They ended up in the playroom, armed with brooms, vacuum cleaner, and dust mops, though

Patty protested piteously that nobody would notice the dust and they really should be washing and setting their hair so they could fix it properly for the company.

"To work!" Natalie told Patty sternly. And Patty knew there was no appeal from that tone of voice.

It was a neat playroom when the guests began to dribble in a few hours later. And Patty and Cathy were both wearing a new hair style and similar sweater-and-skirt outfits in pretty pastels. Patty had taken care to fasten her bracelet well inside her sleeve this time.

Murmurs of astonishment and delight came from the arriving guests as they were met by the look-alikes.

They were all properly puzzled, just as Patty had hoped they'd be, and made quite a happy fuss over it.

It was Yvonne, the pretty redhead, who decided that there had been enough exclaiming about the marvelous resemblance between Patty and her cousin. She put on the latest and loudest record and started snapping her fingers and singing the words along with the record. Her boyfriend, Earl, swung her out to dance, and before Patty realized what was happening, she and Cathy were standing alone, while the young guests went through their gyrations.

"Wh-what do you call this one?" Cathy asked over the shrieking music.

"I dunno. It's new." Patty frowned. "Gee, I wonder what's keeping Richard? He said he'd bring his new car around early."

Just then she heard three loud blasts from a car horn. Patty gave a squeal of excitement. "Hey, everybody, come an' see Richard's new car!"

There was momentary confusion, but within a couple of seconds all four of the boys who had been dancing had abandoned their partners and were hurrying to the door.

"Let's go take a look!" Patty called to the girls, and started to follow the boys. But Cathy was the only one who went with her.

From the basement entrance, Patty caught her first glimpse of the car. It stopped her in her tracks. "Ugh!" she said, clutching Cathy's arm. "That's a *car?*"

At the curb, Richard grinned with pride as he sat at the wheel of one of the most broken-down old jalopies Patty had ever seen. It had wheels, she could see, and at one time it had been a horrible shade of mauve which was now worn off in large patches. It was not what Patty had been visualizing as Richard's new car.

But up front, where the boys were eagerly lifting the hood to get a look at the engine, it was evidently a different story. As the boys gathered around to stare into its depths, Patty and Cathy heard Earl exclaim, "Boy, oh, boy! She's a real heap!"

And Jerry told Richard, as the latter swung out of his seat and swaggered up to join them in admiring his new possession, "Gosh, all you gotta do is fix up the chassis a bit, an' you'll have the keenest set of wheels in town!"

"Yeah," Richard agreed, with his usual brilliance.

"That's *all?*" Patty said with a groan and drew

Cathy back into the hallway with her. "He told me it was a super-duper car and I believed him! It's right out of Noah's Ark."

"The others seem to think it has something," Cathy consoled her. "Maybe it's better than it looks."

"I don't believe it. They're just being polite. Richard's captain of the football squad, you know." Patty was steeped in gloom.

Yvonne and Kerry had come up behind them. "My goodness," Yvonne said, peering over Patty's shoulder, "what on earth is that? I thought you said Richard had a new *car!*"

"Looks like he needs glasses!" Blond Kerry tittered. "First thing you know, he'll be getting you and Cathy mixed up!"

"Don't be silly!" Patty squelched her. "He'd never."

"Does he know you look alike?" Yvonne asked.

"N-No," Patty admitted. "I thought it would be fun to surprise everybody this afternoon."

"Well, then—why don't you play a trick on Richard? Let him see Cathy first and then you come in—" Yvonne plotted. "I bet he'd be fooled."

"Uh, no." Patty shook her head. "We'll come in at the same time." Then she grinned and added, "And you'll see."

A few minutes later, when Richard came in, swaggering a bit, Patty and Cathy were not in the playroom. All the other girls were there, waiting expectantly.

Richard looked around, puzzled. "Hey, where's Patty?"

"Patty!" Kerry called out loudly. "Your big moment's looking for you!" Then she pretended to busy herself picking out a record, while Yvonne and the other two stifled their giggles and waited.

Two doors opened at the same time.

The Patty in one doorway called out, "Hi, Richard!"

"Oh, hi!" Richard waved.

Then a voice made him turn toward the other door. "Hi, Richard!" It spoke in exactly the same tones. Richard's jaw dropped at the sight of a second Patty.

"Holy smoke!" He gasped. "There's two of them!"

The other girls burst into laughter and giggles as Richard looked from one Patty to the other in stupefaction.

"Which one is Patty, Richard?" Yvonne called out.

Richard pulled at his forelock and hesitated. Everyone was staring at him expectantly. He studied both girls. A suspicious bulge on one sweater-cuffed wrist took his eye. He strode suddenly over to one of the girls and threw his arms around her and gave her a quick hug. But the kiss he aimed at her face missed its mark, because Cathy was struggling to free herself.

"I'm Cathy!" she told him, breaking loose.

"You are not!" Richard said, annoyed. "You can't fool me." And before she could back away he had grabbed her by the sleeve and was pulling up the cuff to look for the bracelet he was sure he'd find—the one he had given Patty.

But the bracelet he saw was a plain gold one and not the same at all. He stared at it in amazement and backed off, looking foolish. And when he looked over toward the real Patty she was glaring at him. And everyone but himself and the two cousins was getting a good laugh out of his mistake.

"Oh, gosh, Patty—" he began, starting toward her. But Patty sniffed and turned away. She walked over to the record player and switched it on. Then she looked over at Aaron, the only unattached young man in the room at the moment, and said, "Hey, Aaron, what was that new thing you learned at the Teen Club last night?"

And Aaron, eager to show off, hurried over and led Patty out on the floor while the music brayed and the shocked Richard stared in disbelief. *His* steady date walking out on him just because he'd made a little mistake!

Richard's face turned crimson and he stalked back to Cathy. "How about showing up a couple of amateurs?" he asked loudly enough for everyone to hear. "Let's go, doll."

Cathy started to back away, smiling politely. "I'm sorry—"

Richard leered at her. "I wasn't so dumb. I bet you can dance circles around her." And before Cathy could answer, he whirled her out on the floor and was going into an exaggerated twist and twirl number.

Several of the others applauded. "Go to it, Rich!" Earl called out, laughing, as Richard whirled Cathy around dizzily.

Cathy struggled, panting. "Please, I'm afraid I don't know how—" But Richard cut off her protests with another dizzy whirl-around. It left Cathy staggered, and even Richard himself a little walleyed, though he tried to go on.

And then, to cap it all, Richard stepped squarely on her foot. Cathy gave a yelp of pain that she could not suppress, and pushed him away violently. "You—oaf!" she said angrily and hurried away.

The record ground raucously to a finish as Richard stood looking foolish in the middle of the floor while Cathy limped over to a chair and sat down, nursing her instep.

No one had anything to say for a moment.

Then Richard suddenly bolted from the room. He let the front door slam after him.

Patty made a gesture as if to follow him, then turned back to the others, who were watching uncomfortably. "Let's try a shag!" she said as gaily as she could. And a moment later she had changed the records and her guests were dancing again.

But Patty, hurrying toward Cathy, heard a motor roar down the street and then gradually die away. She sat down beside Cathy. "Well, he's gone," she said flatly, toying with the token bracelet as she spoke.

Cathy looked unhappy. "Oh, Patty! I shouldn't have been so rude. But my foot hurt horribly!" She looked at Patty's set face. "Should I call him at home and apologize?"

Patty turned to Cathy and tried to smile. She patted her cousin's hand and said confidently, "I should say not! He'll do the phoning. And I expect to hear from him before dinner!"

4   *"Spook Castle"*

Long after all the guests had gone and the play-room was neat again, Richard still hadn't called.

The phone had rung several times, and Patty had dashed to answer it. But each time it had been for her father or mother.

And then Ross made things worse by reporting that as he walked home from Davey's house, he saw Richard driving a purple jalopy full of guys and surfboards toward the beach.

"They were sure whoopin' it up, too," he added for good measure, "yellin' at some girls on the sidewalk."

Ross snickered when his sister developed a sudden headache at that piece of information. They were just in the midst of dinner at the moment, but Patty had a sudden loss of appetite, asked hastily to be excused, and left the dining room with the air of Marie Antoinette courageously going off to the guillotine.

"What, may I ask, is the tragedy this time?" Martin inquired when the door had closed softly behind his elder child.

Natalie turned to Cathy, who was gazing sympathetically after her cousin. "I suppose it's a dire secret, so I won't ask you what's going on, but if there's anything her poor, ignorant parents can do to cheer her, do let us know."

Cathy hesitated, but Ross spoke up with a knowing chuckle. "Aw, I heard Yvonne an' Kerry talkin' about Richard an' Patty havin' a rumpus. That's what's bitin' her."

"Oh, well," Martin said, relaxing, "if that's the molehill, we can forget it. Let's just be happy to think that our refrigerator won't be raided again for a couple of days by that two-legged termite."

But Martin wasn't really as hardhearted as he pretended to be. A short time later, as he and Cathy were about to start out to call on Mr. Trevett and return the necklace, he saw his daughter sitting disconsolately on the top step of the stairs, watching. He called out, "Don't look so heartbroken, Lady Jane Grey. Grab a bonnet and come along."

Patty was radiant in a flash. "Yipes! Be with you in two shakes!" She disappeared toward her room, but a brief moment later she was back, dangling her best cashmere sweater by one sleeve and leaping downstairs two steps at a time, as usual.

It was only a few blocks to the corner where the tall old mansion sat in elderly elegance in its well-kept gardens. It commanded a handsome view of the distant Manhattan skyline to the north, the busy wharves and the shining river below the bluff, and the great bridge that spanned the river.

Now, as evening shadowed the scene, lights were beginning to appear in the tall towers of the city and thousands more twinkled from the giant cables of the bridge.

The trio stopped for a long, admiring look before they turned in at the ornate iron gate of the picket fence with its sharp, forbidding spikes.

They went up the ancient brick walk that was

bordered with neatly trimmed privet hedges. The only modern touch visible at the moment was the driveway that had its own entrance and ended at some invisible garage at the rear.

The big front doors were opened by a prim, gray-haired maid who led them through a small foyer into a huge reception hall with a marble floor and a few pieces of antique furniture arranged formally against the walls. A handsome chandelier was suspended from the high ceiling, its prisms glittering like diamonds. An impressive great staircase wound down from the floor above.

"I'll tell Mr. Trevett you have arrived," the maid told Martin. "Please be seated." Then she hurried up the broad stairway and disappeared down a hallway that opened off the balcony.

"Why wasn't I born rich instead of beautiful?" Patty asked with a huge sigh, looking around appreciatively before she plopped down on one of the fragile gilt chairs. The chair teetered and Martin looked alarmed.

"Take it easy there, chicken," he warned.

"Break that and the whole family goes on a diet of bread and water for the next year to pay for it!"

"Oops!" Patty got up in a hurry. "Guess I'd rather stand anyhow!" She turned to Cathy who had seated herself sedately on a twin of the chair. "Let's look around."

"I hardly think that's safe, either," her father said.

"We won't touch a thing, honestly," Patty assured him earnestly. "I just want to peek into that room."

"Well, OK, but come back in a minute or so," her father conceded. "And, Cathy, smack her hand if she tries to pick up anything!"

Cathy nodded, her eyes twinkling. "You can count on me, Uncle Martin." Then she got up quickly and hurried to join Patty. They disappeared into the next room.

Martin closed his eyes and sighed. "No crashes, please," he whispered hopefully. Then he went back to admiring the great chandelier and was tempted to count the prisms.

Patty suddenly popped into sight at the doorway. "Dad!" she whispered urgently. "Come look what we found!"

"Ugh! I knew it! What did you break?" he asked, getting up and striding across the marble floor. "I told you—" By that time he had reached the doorway, and as Patty pointed, he looked at what was in the room and was silenced. He went in slowly.

The room was softly lighted and somewhat in shadow at the far end. But there was no mistaking what it was that extended from the solid wall and well into the room. It was the bow of a sailing ship with a beautifully carved and tinted form of a young girl as its figurehead. Above this, the splintered end of the bowsprit projected a yard or two farther into the room.

The illusion was that the remainder of the ship was still somehow imprisoned beyond the wall.

"It looks like the real thing," Martin told the girls.

"It is, indeed, Mr. Lane," a voice said from behind them. The speaker was a spry little old man with a shock of snow-white hair and bright blue eyes. He stood smiling at them as he switched on the lights in the room.

"Mr. Trevett!" Cathy hurried to him and he took both her hands as he smiled into her eyes.

"Dear Cathy!" he said. "I am so happy to see you again." And as Cathy introduced Patty and Martin, he welcomed them heartily.

"I hope you'll excuse us for snooping about, sir," Martin Lane began.

"Delighted you did," Trevett chuckled. "Jessie Belle here has probably been wishing for company. She's been shut up here in the dark much too long."

"A beautiful bit of carving," Martin Lane said, going closer to examine the figurehead. "I suppose there's a bit of history here."

"Quite so, Mr. Lane." The old gentleman admitted the fact, smiling.

"Please tell us about it," Patty said. "Was this part of a real ship?"

"The finest of our merchant fleet. But she went down in a typhoon in the China Sea over a hundred years ago, and all hands were lost, including Captain Jonas Trevett and his pretty young daughter, Jessie Belle, the one that the ship was named after." He smiled up at the figurehead. "They say Captain Jonas paid a real artist a large sum to carve that likeness and he did a good job."

"She must have been very pretty," Cathy said softly.

Patty was more practical in her reaction. "If the ship went down away over in China, how did this get back here?"

"It floated ashore on a small island a few weeks after the wreck. Jessie's brother Ahab, who tells about it in his diary that I have in the library, found it. He had it shipped home."

"That seems like a strange thing to do," Cathy said. "Especially having it mounted in the wall like this. Why did they do that?"

"Ahab's diary says he had it done for Jessie Belle's mother. The poor lady had gone out of her mind brooding over the disaster, and when she saw the figurehead, she seemed to believe it was Jessie Belle come home to her. He wrote that

she came and sat for hours here, talking to Jessie
Belle's likeness, and thinking her daughter spoke
to her." He sighed. "And maybe she did! Ahab
didn't tell, but it could be. Yes, indeed, it could
very well be." He winked at Martin Lane and
chuckled as Patty's eyes grew round with excitement.

"They say there've been some strange noises
heard from time to time up in the picture gallery
where Jessie Belle's portrait is hanging." He
went on. "Heard a few myself when I was a young
one." He chuckled. "Could 'a' been our Jessie."

"Uncle Owen, *please!*" The stout, pleasant-
faced woman smiled indulgently as she came up
to Mr. Trevett and his guests. "You know you're
just saying that to frighten our visitors. There are
no such things as ghosts, and they know it."

"They do, hey? Well, *I* don't!" Owen Trevett
glared at her belligerently. "And neither do a lot
of other people!"

"Oh, I've heard of quite authentic family ghosts
in England, and Ireland, too," Cathy backed him
up quickly.

"There! I told you!" Owen Trevett said to his antagonist.

The woman laughed and made a gesture of surrender. "All right, Uncle Owen; I take it all back. Please don't upset yourself. And do take your guests out of this horribly drafty room before you all catch your death of cold." She turned smilingly to Martin and the girls. "I'm Mira Burton, and I'm trying to take care of my uncle, even though he doesn't seem to want me to!" She shook a finger at him in playful reproach.

"I'm sorry, Mira," Owen Trevett said quickly. "I appreciate all you're doing. I'm just off balance after that plane ride, I guess. This is Cathy, and her uncle and cousin." He turned to them. "My—uh—my *niece*."

"My dear child," Mira Burton gushed, "thank you a million times for your kindness to my uncle on that dreadful plane trip! Believe me, I shall see that he never has to travel alone again!" And as she finished speaking, she drew Cathy to her and kissed her on the cheek before Cathy had a chance to duck. Then she turned to Patty. "And what a remarkable resemblance between you two!" She made a move as if to kiss Patty, too, but Patty sidestepped briskly and foiled her. Mira Burton's smile faded noticeably. She gave Patty a hard look. "Well, dears," she said quickly, "I'll order some tea and cakes for you, if you'll excuse me now." And a moment later, she was rustling away in the direction of the kitchen.

"We just had dinner," Martin Lane said apologetically to his host. "I'm afraid we won't have room for tea and cakes."

Owen Trevett sighed. "I've only been home a couple of days, and I've found out there's no use arguing with her."

"I couldn't eat a bite," Patty said firmly.

"Nor I," Cathy concurred.

"Perhaps I'd better just give you the necklace and we'll leave before she comes back," Martin Lane suggested, bringing the jewel case out of his pocket and proffering it to Mr. Trevett.

The old gentleman seemed crestfallen and was reluctant to take it. "It's Cathy's now. I gave it to her and I never take things back."

"But she's just a child. Something might happen to it long before she could wear it and feel comfortable in anything so valuable," Martin Lane reminded him.

"That's right, Mr. Trevett," Cathy agreed. "I'd worry about it a great deal. Please take it back."

"I won't," he said stubbornly. Then he had an idea. "But I'll keep it in my safe for you until you are old enough to wear it. And I'll see that there's a paragraph added to my will saying that the necklace belongs to you. Will that do?"

"I suppose—if you insist," Cathy agreed. And Martin Lane approved.

Patty sighed regretfully when the necklace disappeared into the library safe. Five years was a long time to wait to borrow it. But Mr. Trevett cheered her with a suggestion that the two girls go to the portrait gallery on the upper floor to look at Jessie Belle's portrait, done a century or more ago. He was very proud of it.

"She's a lovely lass," he told them. "Be sure to cover her portrait again before you come down. I wouldn't have her catch a cold." And he

chuckled as he saw their surprised expressions.
"And here, take these flashlights in case the
candles flicker out."

"No electricity?" Patty asked.

"My father would have none of it. Too dan-
gerous, he said," the old gentleman explained
with a pixie twinkle. "So it's candles or nothing.
But use the flashlights, and Papa will never
know!"

They found the long gallery dark and spooky.
The full-length portrait of Jessie Belle was draped,
just as were the others. They found her as lovely
as Owen Trevett had claimed her to be. There
was even a likeness to the figurehead downstairs.
But it was her dainty little feet in their gilded
slippers that they both exclaimed over.

Cathy sniffed suddenly. "I smell tobacco smoke.
Ugh!"

"So do I," Patty agreed.

They flashed their lights around, but there was
no one to be seen. The few antique chairs along
the walls and a couple of larger pieces were draped
with dust covers, but nothing moved. Then

Cathy's light fixed on a fireplace near the windows. "It's probably coming up from below," she said, "through the damper."

Just as she spoke, they heard a strange moaning sound from the other end of the room. Patty grasped Cathy's arm. "Did you hear that?"

"A shutter creaking," Cathy said bravely.

"Oh-o-oh!" They heard it again—a shivery sound, not like a shutter.

That was enough for Patty. She dropped her flashlight and bolted through the doorway.

Cathy tried to stop her but missed her grasp. "Wait, Patty!" she called.

But Patty called back, "Stay if you want to! I'm leaving!" She darted for the stairs.

Cathy heard the moan again and gave up. She ran toward the door. But as she reached it, she dropped her flashlight and had to stop and pick it up. It was then that she heard an unmistakable snicker coming from behind her in the dark gallery. Someone was playing games.

5   *Byron*

By that time, Patty was halfway down the second flight of stairs.

Cathy closed the gallery door firmly behind her and then dashed downstairs to overtake Patty. "Wait!" she called in a stage whisper.

Patty waited at the foot of the stairs, a bit uneasily.

"We needn't have panicked," Cathy told her with a smile. "There's someone hiding up there. I distinctly heard a snicker as I was closing the door."

"Who'd be there?" Patty asked suspiciously. "Especially *snickering!*"

"I have one guess," Cathy admitted with a little giggle. "You told your dad that Ross found his way in here once. He may have followed us tonight, just to show us he could do it again."

"I bet you're right!" Patty said indignantly.

"I'm going to go back up there—" She broke off and clutched her cousin's arm, looking up the stairway. "Someone's walking around up there," she whispered.

Cathy heard it, too—the sound of footsteps starting down from the upper story.

"If it's Ross, let's give ol' snoopy the surprise of his life," Patty whispered. "We'll duck into one of these rooms and jump out as he's going by!"

They slipped into the nearest room and closed the door except for an inch or two through which they watched for him. Patty had a hard time suppressing her giggles as they listened to the footsteps descending the stairs.

"Get ready to say 'Boo!' " Patty whispered. But a moment later she pulled back, stifling a gasp of surprise.

It wasn't Ross at all out there. It was a stranger. A very good-looking young man a couple of years older than they were. He was slim and had slicked-down dark hair combed in the newest style approved by the high school set. And to top all else, his clothes were the latest style in sports outfits.

He was smiling to himself, and just as he moved past, unaware of his observers, he gave a snicker of amusement that indignant Cathy recognized as similar to the one she had heard in the gallery.

They both waited until they heard him go down the next flight and enter one of the rooms on that floor. Then Cathy frowned and said, "I wonder who *he* is."

"Who cares?" Patty rolled her eyes and clasped her hands to her heart. "Just so we get to meet him! Wasn't he *gorgeous?*"

Cathy wrinkled her nose in disdain. "If you like boot polish on the hair."

"I wouldn't care *what* he used," Patty gurgled. She pulled Cathy into the hall. "Let's find out what he's doing here in Grant's Tomb!"

They tiptoed down past the closed door. They could hear someone whistling inside one of the rooms, and as they moved by, Patty pretended to swoon against the wall. Cathy jerked her along, not the least amused, and still annoyed at the trickster.

They were halfway down the lower stairs,

when Cathy put out her hand and stopped her cousin. She quietly drew her attention to Mrs. Burton, standing silently with tea tray in one hand and a plate of cakes in the other. She was listening to something going on in the library, and her expression was angry and resentful as she leaned close to the door.

Patty suppressed a giggle, but a tiny part of it escaped and called Mrs. Burton's attention to them. For a brief moment, she scowled resentfully at them, but then she smiled blandly and asked, "Would one of you girls please open the door for me? I have my hands full."

They went to her assistance, and she hurried on into the library with the tea and cakes, bustling up to Mr. Trevett and Martin Lane at the fireplace.

"Come, everyone, and have some of Teresa's delicious little cakes. The poor old dear was too sleepy to serve them herself, so I sent her to bed and played maid for you myself!" She laughed a little too heartily.

Cathy raised an eyebrow at Patty, and Patty

winked at her knowingly.

"You needn't have bothered, Mira," old Mr. Trevett told her with a frown, and he declined both tea and cakes.

Mira Burton looked annoyed; then her expression changed. She became reproachful. "Very well, Uncle Owen. I suppose it is rather late for you to take anything, so close to the time you should be thinking of going to bed."

"Oh, come now, Mom." A voice spoke from the doorway. "You can't bully Uncle Owen the way you do me! He's over twenty-one."

The young man whom the girls had seen upstairs leaned lazily in the doorway a moment longer, while Mira's face went red. Patty stared, fascinated, and Martin looked surprised.

"Right, Byron!" The pixie grin flashed across the old gentleman's face. "Come in and meet our guests."

"Anytime, Uncle Owen," the brash young man answered and moved over with a swagger. But while he was being introduced to the two girls, his mother left rather abruptly.

"I'm afraid we've hurt your mother's feelings," Trevett said, looking after her. "Better go tell her that we both apologize." He frowned at the boy disapprovingly.

Byron snapped his fingers carelessly. "Oh, she's just pouting a little. She's really a good sport, Uncle Owen." But he soon went out.

Patty looked after him and sighed. "Gee! He's sharp!"

Cathy shook her head. "Not half as sharp as he thinks he is."

The two men were deep in a quiet discussion across the room. The girls heard Owen Trevett say, "It sounds like a splendid idea, Lane. I'll be waiting to hear what your publisher thinks of it. Let me know as soon as you can."

"You can count on that!" Martin told him.

"Wonder what Dad and Mr. Trevett are cooking up? Must be something important or Dad wouldn't have to get Mr. Castle's opinion. Mostly, he writes whatever he pleases for the paper." Patty was very proud of her dad.

"You'll probably hear all about it on the way

home," Cathy assured her. "Oh, here comes that dull character, Byron, again."

Byron sauntered in and plopped down into a chair near them, reaching for the cakes. "Heard you went to look for Jessie Belle's ghost," he said casually. "Any luck?"

Patty looked at him reproachfully and was about to speak, when Cathy said sweetly, "I'm afraid not. Someone tried to scare us, but it was the worst imitation ghost I've ever heard. Quite pathetic, in fact."

Byron scowled and sank down in his chair. Whatever he had intended to say stayed unsaid as he crammed a cake into his mouth.

"I think it's time we were going, girls." Martin Lane called out across the big room, getting to his feet. "Come say good-night."

"Do come again soon," the little old gentleman said cordially, holding a hand of each as they thanked him for the cakes and tea. "I'm sure Byron will be glad to see youngsters his own age around this quiet old place. Won't you, Byron?" He waited pointedly for Byron to agree.

"Yeah, sure," Byron agreed. "Call you some-time, Patty."

"Fine!" Patty beamed. "Maybe you can come to our beach party next weekend! Surfing and swimming and a wienie roast. Love to have you."

"Oke. I'll make the scene," Byron promised lightly.

A few minutes later the three Lanes were strolling homeward along the quiet streets.

Martin Lane hummed to himself and smiled as he strode along. "Come along, lazy ones," he told the girls who had fallen back a few feet to look across the river at a passing liner, ablaze with lights.

They hurried a little, but Cathy turned to look back at the passing ship. She felt suddenly lonely for her father and wished she were on that ship, headed for wherever he was, Africa or anywhere else.

Patty was speaking, softly so that her father wouldn't hear. "Now I wish Richard wouldn't phone and try to make up till after the beach party. The kids will be green-eyed when they see me arrive with Byron. I'm sure he's eighteen-and-a-half at least."

Cathy frowned. "It was a childish trick he played on us, eighteen-and-a-half or not. If anyone should ask my opinion, my choice of the two would be Richard."

"But he isn't glamorous like Byron."

"Glamour could wear off in a hurry if there were a mean streak under it!" Cathy said firmly.

"Oh, Cathy! Don't be so serious!" Patty laughed suddenly. "I'm not planning to *marry* Byron! I just want Richard to know that I'm not droopy over him. I want him to see me dashing around with a real live heir to millions!"

Martin had stopped to let them catch up with him. "What millions?" he teased his daughter.

"Mr. Trevett's," Patty told him pertly. "We were talking about Byron Burton."

"I'm afraid you're barking up the wrong tree, Pattycake. Owen Trevett is a long way from being a millionaire," Martin said seriously. "He owns that big old barn of an antique and what's inside of it. That's all. And it's mortgaged heavily."

"Oh, that's a shame, Uncle Martin," Cathy was quick to say. "No wonder he had to hurry home."

"Wouldn't you just know it?" Patty said in disgust.

"I wish we could do something to help him," Cathy told Martin. "Whatever will become of the dear little old man?"

"That's something in which I'm planning to take a hand," Martin told her. "It isn't all worked out at the moment in here"—he tapped his forehead—"but it's starting to bubble! Just keep your toes and fingers crossed till I have a talk with J. R. tomorrow morning." With that he took an arm of each and stepped out with the two of them at such a merry pace that they arrived home completely out of breath.

The front door opened suddenly as they reached the top step, three abreast and all somewhat breathless.

Natalie greeted them eagerly. "What was it like in Spook Castle, you lucky people? I've chewed off my pet fingernail waiting to hear!"

"We saw some stunning antiques, Aunt Natalie," Cathy told her eagerly. "You must see them!"

"And there was a ship coming right out of a wall," Patty added. Then she asked abruptly, "Any phone calls?"

"Nary a one," Natalie told her, "and it's time both of you turned in. We're going to have a full day sight-seeing tomorrow. So scoot up to bed!"

"OK, Mom," Patty agreed and went quietly upstairs. "G'night."

Her parents looked after her in some surprise,

having expected at least some protest.

Cathy leaned to whisper to Natalie. "Richard." And Natalie nodded her understanding. Then Cathy said good-night and hurried upstairs after her cousin to give her whatever support or comfort she might need.

"And now," Natalie told her husband, "tell me all about Mr. Trevett. Is he such a darling, as Cathy seems to think? And what happened about the necklace? And did you get a chance to snub that snippety nurse who didn't want you to call?"

"Whoa! One thing at a time!" Martin laughed and led the way into his study where they settled themselves. "Where do you want me to begin?" he asked.

"The necklace, of course!" Natalie said promptly. "Where is it?"

"Safe in Trevett's possession till Cathy's of age," he said. "Then she takes it. It will be covered legally in his will."

"Wonderful!" Natalie glowed. "He *must* be a very nice man."

"He's a bit of a pixie along with it," Martin chuckled. "And that 'nurse' turned out to be a niece, after all. Not *his* niece, though. His wife's stepbrother's niece—no real relation at all, though he and his wife have been supporting her and her young son Byron in luxury all their lives."

"I suppose with his millions he didn't mind doing it," Natalie guessed.

But Martin informed her that Owen Trevett was far from being rich. He had only the old mansion and its grounds remaining. The cost of twenty-odd years of travel in search of a cure for his wife's ill health had dissipated his fortune completely, and it had never been as large as gossip claimed it to be. He could barely meet his taxes now.

"After Mrs. Trevett died," Martin went on, "he sent word to this niece that he could no longer give her a large allowance. Almost at once he had a cable telling him that she would give up her home and come to live at his house and take care of him."

"That was thoughtful of her," Natalie said admiringly.

"*He* didn't think so," Martin said wryly. "He cabled her to stay where she was and he'd try to send her a small allowance each month. But that didn't stop her."

"You mean, she moved in after *that?*" Natalie was a bit shocked.

Martin nodded grimly. "And took over. Yesterday he found out that she had been negotiating, without his permission, with a syndicate of apartment house builders for the sale of the property. She had represented herself to them as being qualified to act as agent for the sale. They had made a rather large offer for the place, one that she felt 'Uncle Owen' would be foolish to turn down."

Natalie exclaimed indignantly, "Apartment house builders! But the Trevett mansion is a landmark. It's one of the oldest we have."

"I know. Mr. Trevett wasn't happy about the idea of selling, but he does need money badly—especially with her on his hands now—and he finally had to give in and agree that he'd see Gram-mand and Larch, the builders, some day soon."

"But *apartments!* It's a shame. We've lost so many lovely old landmarks lately to so-called progress!" Natalie moaned.

"We haven't lost this one yet, my girl!" Martin said, flashing a big grin. "I may have an answer for Mr. Trevett! He thinks so, and so do I!"

"Quick, tell me, before I chew off another fingernail!"

"All it needs is J. R.'s cooperation and a series of my hard-hitting, to-the-point editorials for which I am justly famous—" He ducked in time to avoid a memo pad that came flying at him. "OK, I'll talk, officer!"

"You'd better!"

"You remember Williamsburg, Virginia?"

"Of course. You took us there last summer. I adored it. All those quaint old places, restored just as they must have looked back in Colonial days, with people in those old costumes and some of them hard at work making things of Colonial days. Why?"

"Why? Because there's no reason why Brooklyn Heights can't have something like that, only on a smaller scale—centered around the Trevett Mansion, the best-preserved relic of Dutch Colonial days. And filled with authentic antiques, too. Wait till you see that ship's figurehead poking out into a big room just as if it had come crashing through. And the story that goes with it— Well, I could sit down and write that first editorial right now!"

"It sounds terrific!" Natalie said enthusiastically. But a moment later she frowned. "Who's going to pay for the property?" She ticked it off on her fingers. "The state? County? City?"

"The city, I hope!" Martin grinned boyishly. "*If* I can persuade J. R. to use his influence on our city council, and my editorials wake the boys up to the publicity value of the idea, both to Brooklyn Heights and themselves—"

"You mean names on a bronze plaque on the front door of the Trevett mansion. That sort of publicity?" Natalie guessed innocently, tongue in cheek.

"Exactly!" Martin agreed. "Do you think it can fail?"

"Does it ever?" Natalie asked saucily.

There were many handsomely furnished and decorated suites in the Trevett house, and Mira Burton had chosen two of the finest for herself and for Byron. Luxury was something she had always craved.

But at the moment, she was tramping back and forth over the priceless rugs, ignoring their value. Mira was angry—and worried.

Byron was sprawled in careless comfort on a satin-covered antique sofa before the tiled fireplace. He lazily watched his mother through a haze of cigarette smoke.

"Put down that cigarette and pay attention to me," she said sharply, "and sit up like a man."

Byron hastily stubbed out the cigarette and sat up straight, scowling. "I don't know why you've got the wind up," he whined. "All you heard was that newspaper bird Lane saying Uncle Owen ought to sell this creaky old mausoleum to the city for some kind of museum. What do we care who he sells it to, just so he gets a bundle for it? Wasn't that the idea of coming here in the first place, to get some of the loot when you talked him into selling?"

"Don't be common, Byron!" Mira snapped. "Your language is disgusting! And besides, you are stupid! The city pays as little as possible for property of this sort, and all we'd get would be a miserably small allowance from Uncle Owen. If Grammand and Larch buy it—" She hesitated to tell him. This was something she hadn't mentioned.

"Mom!" Byron chortled, jumping up and grabbing her hands with more animation than he had shown all evening. "You've made a deal with them! How much? You slicker!"

Mira frowned and tried to pull her hands away. "Stop that silliness this instant! Of course, I made a deal. A perfectly fair one. A percentage. I felt I'd be entitled to it for my trouble getting Uncle Owen to agree to sell. There's nothing wrong about that."

"I should say there isn't!" Byron rejoiced. "Just so it comes to enough to get me a fast set of wheels and a dash of wardrobe now and then."

"It will." His mother assured him. "Unless this newspaperman Lane puts over his ridiculous ideas and cheats us out of what rightfully should be coming to us!"

"Maybe if Grammand and Larch raised their offer it could make a difference," Byron suggested shrewdly.

"I'm afraid they won't. It took a lot of talking to get them to agree to pay even as much as they finally settled on as the absolute top price," she told him glumly.

"Well, there's no use getting all steamed up about it so soon, Mom," Byron said lazily. "So far, we don't even know if Lane was just talking, or if he could put over his idea anyhow. He may be a bag of wind."

"It's possible. I mustn't panic," Mira said firmly. "But if he really means to go ahead with that ridiculous scheme, I'll do everything I possibly can to stop it!"

"There's just one thing," Byron said carefully. "If I were you, I wouldn't come out and sound off against it when Uncle Owen brings it up. Play it cool!"

"Nonsense! I shall tell him exactly what I think," she retorted.

"You do," Byron said in warning, "and the old boy will get his back up. He's not too happy to have us sponging off him as it is, and you'd better try some honey and molasses on him instead of trying to drive him!"

Mira Burton paced the floor, thinking it over. It would be hard to resist telling off Owen Trevett, but perhaps Byron was right. There was no use antagonizing the old fool.

"All right," she said finally. "I'll try to be careful what I say to him, but it isn't going to be easy."

"Good gal!" her son told her impudently. "We'll get that fat commission yet!"

"Indeed we will!" Mira told him firmly.

Over at the Lane house, Cathy and Patty were getting ready for bed. Cathy had just finished writing a letter to her father.

"I told Dad we were going to explore Uncle Martin's offices and watch them printing the *Daily Chronicle* tomorrow," Cathy told Patty happily.

Patty, gazing at herself in the mirror, was experimenting with a swept-high hairdo that didn't seem to be working out as it should. "Oh, gosh!" She moaned as it collapsed for the steenth time and fell down over her eyes. "It won't stay put."

Cathy, brushing her own shoulder-length hair carefully stroke by stroke, came over to watch. "I like it better the way you always wear it," she said quietly.

"But it's too childish," Patty pouted. "I bet the girls Byron Burton knows don't have to fix their hair in kid styles." She gave a hard tug at a strand that was giving her trouble and scowled at herself in the mirror. "And they probably use lipstick lots darker than Mom lets me have."

"Why should you let that worry you?" Cathy asked frankly. "You probably won't be seeing him very often."

Then she saw Patty's ID bracelet that Richard had given her. It was lying on Patty's dressing table. Cathy picked it up and dangled it. "Oh, you took this off."

Patty nodded vigorously, and Cathy noticed that she was smiling a very smug little smile. "I'm sending it back to Richard tomorrow," she said with a toss of the head, "unless he calls me and apologizes for the way he acted."

"But, Patty—" Cathy began.

"There's no use pleading for him," Patty said firmly. "And, anyhow, I prefer people who are more grown-up!"

Cathy hesitated. "I suppose you mean Byron Burton."

Patty smiled at herself in the mirror. "I could. You noticed how quickly he accepted my invitation to come to the beach party."

"He's probably forgotten it completely by now," Cathy said calmly. "Maybe purposely."

Patty was startled. "Why purposely?"

"Well, you said yourself he's more grown-up than Richard, and it's true. Why would he want to go to a beach party where everyone would be two or three years younger than he is?"

"Then why would he say he'd come?" Patty demanded.

"I don't know but I should guess he might have wished to please his uncle by being friendly to us."

"Oh, gosh! That could be." Patty agreed glumly. "I remember now, he didn't even bother to ask when the beach party was to be. He just said he'd come. Maybe you're right."

And she hadn't much to say as they finished undressing and piled into their beds and settled down for the night.

In the darkness, Cathy sighed. She hoped that she had made the right guess about Byron Burton, and that she and Patty would see very little of him. And she hoped that big, clumsy Richard would phone Patty in the morning and move back into her good graces again.

7   *Wheels Start Turning*

It was along toward morning that Cathy awoke to the sound of a typewriter tapping in her uncle's study. She wondered sleepily if it could have anything to do with the idea he'd been hatching on the way home. "It sounds as if it might be coming through nicely," she told herself. "I do hope so!" Then she fell asleep again.

Natalie and Ross were at the breakfast table the next morning as the two girls raced downstairs to the dining room.

"Where's Dad?" Patty asked. "Cathy heard him working last night! How's his idea about Mr. Trevett?"

"Splendid," her mother said. "At the moment, he is off to the wars, clutching a sheaf of priceless prose in his tired little hand. And this had better not be one of J. R. Castle's disapproving days, or Dad will beat him next time they play golf."

Then as all three clamored to be told about Martin's idea, Natalie explained the restoration plan which was to center around the Trevett mansion. "Dad is sure that if J. R. OK's a campaign to put over the idea with the city council, the *Chronicle* can do it. He wrote a bang-up editorial for the opening blast."

"If anyone can do it," Cathy said enthusiastically, "I'm sure Uncle Martin can! Dad says his editorials are the meat of the *Chronicle*."

Natalie put her finger to her lips. "Sh-h-h! Never let J. R. hear you say that! That's treason. And the Lane family's head might r-r-roll!" She made a clicking sound and ran her fingers across her throat mischievously simulating a beheading.

Cathy and Patty laughed, but Cathy sobered at once and said gravely, "I shall be most careful, Aunt Natalie."

"Good girl! And now if you bright young things will get to your breakfasts, we'll soon be on our way across the bridge for our sight-seeing tour."

"OK, Mom!" Patty answered. Then she hesitated a moment before she turned to Ross, already busily eating. "Ross, honey," she said cajolingly, "if I get any calls while I'm out, will you tell him—I mean, them—that I'll call back as soon as I get home?"

Ross looked at her owlishly through his specs. "Bet he won't call."

Patty frowned and tried to look superior. "I really don't know to whom you are referring, brother dear."

"Ow!" Ross pretended to recoil. "I can't stand grammar so early in the morning. I mean Richard, dopey. Or should I say 'dopey Richard'?"

Patty had an answer ready but the extension phone in the kitchen rang just then, and she dashed to answer it.

They could hear the sound of her voice and a couple of laughs, but when she came back into the dining room, Patty was looking puzzled.

"I hope you were nice to Richard," Natalie said.

"It wasn't Richard," Patty said, frowning. "I guess we had Byron sized up wrong, Cath. That was him—he, I mean, Mom—asking what day we're having the beach party and asking if he can drive us."

Cathy frowned and Natalie looked surprised and pleased. "That's Mr. Trevett's grandnephew you're speaking of, isn't it?" Natalie asked. "Dad said he seemed a quiet boy, but apparently someone here made an impression on him."

"Looks like," Patty admitted, smiling archly. "I told him we were planning on next Saturday for the beach blast, and it was too far ahead to know whose car we'd go in."

"Ha!" Ross grinned at her. "Holding out till you get a look at his car! You don't fool me! You're scared he might show up in a worse old wreck than that bucket of bolts Richard's got!"

"Eat, Ross. And you two, I'll give you just fifteen minutes to finish here and meet me at the garage! By now, Dad must be doing his selling to J. R. and I want to let him take us to lunch to celebrate!"

The trip through the quiet streets of the Heights and into the bustling business district was a con-

stant series of thrills for Cathy. Most of the landmarks they passed, and the old Brooklyn Bridge
that they traveled over, were almost as familiar
to Cathy as if she had seen them before. In a way,
she had. For her father, always homesick for his
birthplace, had talked of them most of her life.
And Martin had often sent his absent brother
snapshots of family visits to the parks and the
Museum, and the other famous spots.

Even the Manhattan skyscraper where the
Daily Chronicle was printed looked familiar. And
as they drew up at the entrance, Martin Lane,
waiting eagerly, looked so much like her father
that Cathy's heart gave an excited leap and she
almost called out in happy recognition.

Martin hurried across the sidewalk to them.
"Where's the most glamorous place you girls can
think of for lunch?" he asked happily. "Name it
and you're on your way! Today we celebrate!"

Natalie exclaimed, "Martin! He liked it!"

"Liked it?" Martin almost shouted. "He went
for it hook, line, and sinker! It's going to be our
big campaign for the summer! And we break the

ice tomorrow with that editorial of mine!"

"Wonderful!" Natalie agreed. "But you'd better hop in and let me zoom out of here before that gendarme I see approaching clips my wings with a citation!"

And a moment later, all excitedly talking at once, they were on their way to the celebration.

Half an hour later, as both Patty and Cathy dawdled over tall parfaits and enjoyed every spoonful, Martin spoke quietly to Natalie. The girls were too eagerly interested in their surroundings to notice.

"I have an odd feeling that Trevett's niece won't approve of the museum idea. In fact, from the way she snapped at me over the phone when I called to tell him that J. R. had given me the green light to start the campaign, I gathered that she's decidedly against it!"

"Perhaps she likes living there among the priceless antiques that Cathy has been describing to me," Natalie guessed, a bit reproachfully. "I would. I'd even like to see them some day."

"In good time, wife!" Martin said with a stern

frown. And Natalie made a face at him.

"Not quarreling, I hope?" Patty finished the last morsel at the bottom of the parfait glass. "If you want to work up a good row, I can put away another yummy while you're busy." She looked hopeful.

"Your mother was needling me, the cruel woman, because we left her home last night!" Martin told her. "What I go through!"

The girls laughed at his long face, and Cathy said consolingly to Natalie, "Never mind, Aunt Natalie. I'm certain dear Mr. Trevett would love to have you call any time and look as long as you like at everything."

"And old sneaky Mrs. Burton might give you tea and cakes!" Patty giggled.

"Why 'sneaky'?" her father asked, puzzled.

They told him and her mother about seeing Mira Burton listening at the library door.

"A charming character," Martin commented dryly, then he added mischievously, "curious like all her sex."

And under a barrage of indignant reproaches,

he laughingly paid the bill and shooed his women-folk past the confectionery counter to the car.

While the girls settled themselves for the trip back to the *Chronicle* office for a tour, Martin spoke quietly to his wife. "I can't figure why Mrs. Burton would resent the old chap's selling the place. A couple of days ago when he arrived, she seemed eager enough for him to do it."

"That's right! You said she had already talked to some people about buying it and had wanted him to see them."

"It could be that she lied to the apartment house people about how important she was, and she resents losing face, as the Chinese say," Martin suggested.

Natalie nodded gravely. "Or she's just simply changed her mind and decided she likes living there."

"Well, I'm afraid that if the old gentleman is as broke as he says he is now, she won't enjoy it very long. He can't afford to keep the place!"

"It's a shame." Natalie sighed. "I hope the city council does something about buying it before they adjourn for the summer."

"If they don't, after the editorial campaign J. R. and I have worked out, they're even tougher and less farsighted than I think they are."

"Isn't the president of the council, Mr. Peterson, a close friend of J. R.?"

"He is, indeed. And he's also a loyal Brooklynite and from a family almost as long-settled here as the Trevetts."

"Well, that's a break for Mr. Trevett," Natalie said happily. "Climb into the chariot and we'll go do the fifty-cent tour of the greatest newspaper in the world."

A few minutes later they sped on to an afternoon of shopping and sight-seeing that kept them busy until dinnertime.

Ross watched the trio limp up the steps to the front door, footsore and weary. He frowned disapprovingly. "Gosh, I'm starved. And I suppose I'll have to wait for dinner till you're rested up."

"A heartless monster," Patty groaned to Cathy.

But Natalie stopped to pat his head as she went by. "Wipe the cookie crumbs off your mouth and have patience, little man!" Then she and Cathy limped inside, arm in arm.

But Patty lingered. "Any calls for me, monster?" She slipped off one shoe and massaged the foot tenderly.

"No calls," he said promptly, "but I did see a guy you used to go steady with last week. What was his name again? That dumb football character?"

"Oh, Richard came by?" She tried to keep from sounding too eager, but Ross looked knowing. She wasn't fooling him.

"Yeah," he said, starting into the house.

"Hold it!" Patty caught him by the sleeve. "What did *he* want?"

"He didn't say. He just drove past."

"Oh," Patty said in a very small voice, letting go of Ross's arm.

But as she moved toward the door, Ross weakened. "He drove past four times, real slow, like he was looking for somebody here."

Patty brightened and her smile flashed. "Thanks! You're really not a bad type for a brother!" And she hopped on into the house feeling much better.

Cathy was stretched out on her bed, face down, and wiggling her toes. "Hi," she said in a voice muffled by the pillow, "be with you as soon as I get the circulation going!"

"Just you rest," Patty said gaily, without a sign of fatigue in her voice. "I'll give Mom a hand on the dinner. I feel great." She kicked off her other shoe and dashed for her bedroom slippers.

Cathy sat up abruptly, staring. "Well, that's a quick recovery, indeed!" she laughed. "I know! Richard's called and everything's patched up!"

But Patty shook her head. "No, but he's weakening! I'm not sending his bracelet back just yet."

When Cathy had heard the details she was inclined to agree with the strategy. Richard might be dull and clumsy, but he was a lot better for Patty to pal around with than Byron, in Cathy's eyes.

"I'm glad," Cathy told her cousin.

"I guess I am, too," Patty admitted, with a grin. "But I still think Byron's neat."

8   *Patty Takes Steps*

Martin Lane's first editorial attack on the money-grubbing of certain building outfits who were tearing down old landmarks proved to be a sensation. Letters started pouring in to the *Daily Chronicle* almost before the ink was dry.

A great many people seemed to feel as Lane and his publisher felt. And when his second editorial mentioned the Trevett mansion—"one of our most cherished relics of the bygone glories of the Heights"—and suggested that it might be next to disappear, the clamor began.

The deluge of indignant letters continued, peppered only occasionally by some which poked fun at the conservative die-hards who were trying to hold back progress.

On his way home the next day, Martin stopped in to show old Mr. Trevett a selection of the letters received.

"Tomorrow," Martin told him, "my editorial will suggest that the city should buy your home and make it the center of a reconstruction project to attract visitors. I think that will appeal to merchants as well as old-line Brooklynites."

"I hope so! I am anxious to be finished here and on my way back to Scotland for good," said the old man as they sat in the library before the fireplace. A small fire flickered, taking the chill off the high-ceilinged room.

"I feel that it won't be long now," Martin assured him. "There's one hurdle, though. The city council is the body that has to decide whether they approve the project or not."

"I would think that if enough citizens care what becomes of their historical heritage, the council should be easy to convince," Trevett said, frowning.

"Council President Peterson believes they will, but it may take some argument. He says that two of the members of the council, Thad Brown and Denker, are hardheaded businessmen who would like to see the entire district given over to high-rise apartment buildings."

"There must be some way to persuade them," Trevett said, bending close to the fireplace to poke the little flame into a livelier blaze. "Perhaps you'll think of something."

"If I don't, Peterson may," Martin told him cheerfully. "There's always opposition to anything, no matter how worthy it is."

"I know," the old gentleman agreed with a sigh. "Take Mira, my dear wife's niece. It won't make any difference to her if I sell to the apartment house people or to the city. I'll still give her the same allowance. But now she's going around moping and resenting my change of plans."

"But why?" Martin asked.

Trevett shook his head. "Claims it's a disgrace to put the family home on public exhibition. Not that it's *her* family home, as I reminded her last night!"

"How did she figure it was a disgrace? Just the opposite, I'd say."

"I don't know how she figured. Just a woman, I guess. Didn't want those apartment house people to know she wasn't the boss of the place, like she'd told them, I suppose." He snorted. "I told her I'd made up my mind to it, and the city was going to have their chance to buy this place before I had any dealings with those builders. And that was that!" He chuckled. "That convinced her and she went off to bed like a martyr going to the lions!"

"She seems to have strong opinions." Martin smiled.

"I'm not letting it bother me," Trevett snapped. "I didn't ask her to come here, and she can leave whenever she wishes to and take that lazy loafer with her."

But Mira Burton had no intention of leaving. She had been called to the offices of Grammand and Larch to explain this sudden switch. Mr. Larch indignantly reminded her that she had agreed, as old Mr. Trevett's representative, to arrange for him to sell his place to them.

"My uncle is absentminded. He's forgotten that he told me I could represent him," she lied firmly.

Karl Larch, frowning, told her sharply, "He sounds more simpleminded to me." He added, "A little childish."

Mira's eyes widened. But a moment later she was hiding a smile under her handkerchief as she dabbed at her eyes and pretended to be deeply moved. "Oh, I do hope—I mean—that side of the family—there has been a weakness, I've heard—oh, nothing *serious*, but—" She broke off, as he stared at her in surprise. Then she hurried on. "But dear Uncle Owen is perfectly all right. He just forgets things."

"Or he wants to play us against the city!" Larch said suspiciously. "Is that it?"

"Certainly not! It's that newspaperman, Martin Lane, who suggested the silly idea of a museum to him!"

Larch frowned over that for a minute or two. Then he said abruptly, "I want that Trevett place. It's the best location for the building we're planning. But there are two other locations almost as good. I could sign for their purchase tomorrow."

"Please! I'm sure I can persuade my uncle to

give up this foolishness. Give me a few days!" Mira insisted.

Larch looked at his desk calendar. "I can give you two weeks at the outside. I must have Trevett's signed agreement to sell to us by that time. I can't wait any longer."

Mira stood up. Her set jaw reflected grim purpose. "You will have it."

Martin Lane came home whistling. "Hi, where's everybody?" he called from the hallway.

Cathy answered promptly by appearing at the study door, book in hand. "Patty's on the phone, I'm reading, and Ross hasn't come from the cinema yet."

"And dinner's ready in the oven, but you're much too late to save the chocolate soufflé. We have to have the bread pudding again for dessert." Natalie, in the rear hallway, laughed at his disappointed face.

"I'm sorry," he said. "I meant to phone, but I forgot. I stopped at Trevett's to leave a pile of letters protesting about letting the property go to the apartment builders. He's delighted."

"He'll probably get hundreds more when they read about the museum project tomorrow," Natalie guessed.

"I hope so! I suggested it would be a good idea to answer them all if he could. Good 'relations'."

"But what a job that would be! He could never do it," Natalie objected, frowning.

"Not unless he had a couple of willing workers to lend a hand," Martin said, with a meaningful look at Cathy. "Or at least one."

"Oh, please, Uncle Martin! May I? I'd be very happy to." Cathy was eager.

"That was sort of what I had in mind. I could drop you off tomorrow morning on my way to work, and—"

Patty interrupted from the doorway of the study. "But, Cathy, we planned to go see the Statue of Liberty tomorrow." She looked annoyed.

"You have all summer ahead of you for that," Martin reminded Patty sternly.

"You won't mind postponing the trip, will you,

Patty?" Cathy asked apologetically. "I'd really like to help Mr. Trevett with the letters."

"Of course, she won't mind," Martin said firmly. "I'll count on you." And he patted his niece's arm approvingly.

"OK," Patty answered shortly. "I can find things to do by myself." And she sank down on the bottom stair and looked tragic, cupping her chin in a palm.

Martin and Natalie exchanged half-amused and half-exasperated glances and then went arm in arm toward the kitchen.

Cathy was troubled. "Really, Patty, we do have lots of time for sight-seeing," she told her cousin. And then she noticed that Patty was wearing the ID bracelet again. "Oh, you put it on again! Richard called and you didn't tell me!" she reproached her playfully.

But Patty shook her head gloomily. "No, he didn't. That was Yvonne, the last call. She says she saw Richard with a red-haired girl in his jalopy—a girl she didn't know. They were laughing and having a ball and they were driving

toward the beach road." She sighed heavily. "It's all over between us."

"It could have been a family friend in the car," Cathy suggested calmly. "Why don't you phone Richard? I'm sure he'd be delighted."

"No! He's got to do the calling," Patty said firmly. But she added with a catch in her voice, "I guess I'll have to mail his old bracelet back to him."

"I'd keep it a bit longer," Cathy advised. "I have a feeling he's going to call you tonight." She sounded reassuring even to herself.

Patty brightened. And she kept the bracelet on all evening and hovered close to the phone. But when the call failed to come, she was more downcast than ever and Cathy felt guilty.

In the morning, when Cathy opened her eyes, she was startled to see Patty already dressed and waiting for her.

"I'm going with you. I can help, too," Patty informed her cousin.

"Are you sure you want to?" Cathy asked.

"If you'll put up with my spelling. Sometimes

it's ghastly," Patty admitted gaily. "I'm sick of hanging around the house. And it'll be fun to make believe we're rich and live in that mansion."

But Cathy wasn't at all sure that Patty was being quite frank. There *was* a certain character named Byron!

Martin was surprised and pleased to learn that Patty had volunteered to help. He proudly escorted them to the front door of the mansion and offered to call for them on his way home in the late afternoon.

"Oh, please don't trouble, Uncle Martin!" Cathy said hastily. "It's only a short walk, and I'm sure we'll enjoy it after being closed in all day."

"That's good thinking," Martin told her. He kissed both girls and drove away.

Mrs. Burton received them coldly, but Cathy was gracious in spite of it and thanked her cheerfully. There was no sign of Byron, Cathy was happy to see.

"I hope he's on his way to Timbuktu," she thought to herself. But she noticed that Patty obviously was disappointed at not seeing him and was not very interested in their purpose for being there.

Many more letters came in the morning mail, all urging Owen Trevett not to sell his landmark property. He dictated a friendly answer and both girls set to work making copies.

But after she had finished a handful, Patty wandered around the room, bored. Staying long at any task became a "moth-eaten drag" to Patty. She went to look out of the window and was suddenly alert at sight of a huge, old-fashioned car, gleaming with chromium, being rolled out of the garage by Byron and the old caretaker Mark.

"Hey, come look, Cath!" she called excitedly. "What is that big ol' thing?"

Cathy stopped working to see. "Why, it's a Duesenberg! It must be about thirty years old. One of Dad's friends in London had one almost like it! They're terribly valuable to people who collect antique cars. Worth thousands!"

"Really?" Patty squeaked. "I've got to get a good look at it! Be back in a flash!" And off she went before Cathy had a chance to remind her of the letters. And she still hadn't returned when Cathy had finished the last letter and laid them all neatly on Mr. Trevett's desk to be signed.

She looked out of the window. Old Mark was working on the engine of the big car, and Patty and Byron were visiting cozily, laughing and discussing the many gadgets on its dashboard.

Cathy went back to the desk. Unless Richard stopped being stubborn, he was going to lose out. She reached for the phone.

9 *Mira's Scheme*

"You sure Patty wants me to come pick her up there?" Richard asked suspiciously. "It's funny she can't call me herself!" He was still sulking.

"Silly!" Cathy said gently. "You know how she is. She's dying to see you, but she won't give in and phone. So I'm playing Cupid." She laughed.

"Aw, thanks, Pathy—I mean, Catty—Gosh! I'll be there. Sure hope she likes my new car."

But after he had put down the phone, he scratched his head doubtfully. "Now, did she say come at two or when?" The only figures he was ever sure of were football signals. "Must 'a' been two," he finally decided, because it sounded familiar. Anyhow, if he was early, he'd wait. He never minded waiting for Patty.

Mr. Trevett entered the library as Cathy put down the receiver. "More letters and a handful of telegrams," he said proudly, dumping a load onto the desk. "All in favor!" Then he looked around the room. "Where's our favorite cousin?"

Before Cathy could reply, the roar of the powerful Duesenberg engine filled the library.

When it died down to a low rumble, Mr. Trevett beamed at Cathy and said with a chuckle, "The old dragon still has a roar!" He hurried over to the window and looked down. "I haven't heard that in twenty-five years, but I'd know it anywhere. Always had me a bit scared. Felt as if I had a snortin' bull alligator by the tail when I drove that thing."

Cathy followed him to the window, and was just in time to see Byron driving gingerly down the driveway with Patty beside him and old Mark hobbling alongside, calling out directions as to what to do next.

Owen Trevett chuckled. "I'm sure the young rascal never drove anything that size before!"

But as he spoke, the big car took on speed, and a moment later it had roared out of the driveway and into the quiet street and disappeared.

"Oh, I hope they return safely!" Cathy exclaimed. She added to herself, "And before Richard arrives looking for Patty!"

"Don't worry, youngster," Trevett told her. "The boy says he's driven fast cars before. It's just a case of getting used to the old-fashioned driving gear."

Then he and Cathy went to work sorting out the new letters and composing answers for Cathy and Patty to type.

It was soon lunchtime, and there was still no sign of the pair. Cathy was so worried now that she had no appetite, and when Mira came bustling in to announce that luncheon was ready, Cathy politely excused herself.

When Mr. Trevett had gone, after trying to coax her to come along and eat, Cathy tried to telephone Richard to ask him to come later instead of at three o'clock. But there was no answer at his house.

She was feeling pretty desperate when suddenly she heard the roar of the Duesenberg engine. A moment later she saw the big car turn into the driveway. Patty and Byron seemed quite at home in it as Byron drove smoothly up to the garage and stopped. They were chatting like old friends.

For once, Cathy felt angry with Patty. Then she laughed at herself. Patty had had no way of knowing that Richard would be coming to call for her. And furthermore, this wasn't Patty's task, so she wasn't duty-bound to do a share of it. Cathy prepared to forgive her for running off. But she didn't feel quite so generous toward Byron. She simply could not bring herself to like him.

Old Mark looked with disapproval at the mud-splashed fenders as the two young people alighted from the big car. Then he told Byron, "Kinda gave it a workout, didn't you?"

"It's just mud. You won't have any trouble getting it off," Byron answered impudently.

"I sure enough won't," Mark snapped. "That's your job, sonny. I heard the master tell you about that. You drive it, you keep it shined up. I've got my own work." And he turned and stamped off.

"Why, you—" Byron's face was crimson with

anger, but he swallowed the rest of the remark. Uncle Owen hadn't been very willing to let him take out the old car. He'd better watch his step for a few days.

"Well, thanks for the ride. I hope some of the gang from school saw me!" Patty laughed. "They'll be knocked silly!" She gave a last little wave and started toward the house. But she went only a step or two. Byron took a firm grip on her arm and stopped her.

"You can't walk out on me that way, gal," he told her. "If I have to scrub, I'll need a polisher. And you're elected."

"But I haven't had any lunch." Patty tried to look weak.

"We'll dig something up in the kitchen when we get through. I can't take a chance on dear old Uncle Owen seeing his chariot all muddied up. He might get narrow-minded about letting me use it!"

Patty gave in. "OK," she agreed a little sulkily. "But if I faint from hunger while we're doing it, it's your fault." But all she got in reply was a teasing grin.

A few minutes later, they were both hard at work on the fenders. And Patty, who was really a willing worker when she had to be, was soon chattering at great length about school and plans for Saturday's party at the beach.

Upstairs, Cathy waited impatiently for her cousin. She should be dashing up any moment, full of excitement about her ride. There would still be time to tell her that Richard would be there at three o'clock. She knew Patty would want to get prettied up before he arrived.

But Patty didn't come up. Minutes passed. She could hear Patty laughing from time to time. Byron evidently had what Patty's pals called a "good line."

Cathy made up her mind suddenly to go break up the twosome. Patty had work to do up here. She was starting to the door when she heard another car coming up the driveway. The motor didn't roar like the Duesenberg's. It was noisy and it sputtered and choked.

With a horrible suspicion, she dashed to the window. Her worst fears were realized. It was

Richard's purple jalopy with the owner at the wheel. And he was exactly one hour and fifteen minutes early. And from the look on his face, he had already seen Patty and Byron. He was scowling blackly.

Cathy staggered back to the desk and sank into the chair. "It's all my fault for being Miss Fix-It," she told herself miserably. "I hope they all remember their manners, but something tells me Richard isn't going to be very happy with either Patty or me!"

Below, Richard brought the jalopy to a stop, climbed out and stalked toward Patty. She had a wide smudge of grease on her face and her hair was hanging over one eye. She stood staring at him in amazement. Of all the people she might have expected to see, Richard was certainly the last.

"Hi, Richard," she said with a weak giggle. "Imagine meeting you here."

Byron swaggered up to Richard. "All deliveries at the rear, boy," he said arrogantly.

Richard was puzzled now. He ignored Byron.

"Cathy called and said you'd be ready to leave when I came."

It was a big surprise to Patty. "I didn't know she was going to call."

Byron grabbed the taller boy's sleeve. "Look here, fella," he said patronizingly, "why don't you climb back into that broken-down relic and be on your way?"

Richard looked down at him. "Shoo, kiddy," he said, not unkindly, and shook off Byron's hand. "Keep away." Then he turned again to Patty. "You coming?" he asked grimly.

"No, she isn't! And get out of my driveway!" Byron snarled and picked up a tire iron.

Richard lost his temper then. He put out his arm and swept Byron out of the way, tire iron and all. Unluckily for Byron, he staggered back against the half-emptied water bucket and tripped over flat on his back, sprawling in the dirty water. He looked so funny that Richard couldn't help laughing.

"Richard! How could you hit him?" Patty didn't think it was so funny.

"Didn't hit him," Richard snapped. "Anyhow, he started it."

Byron stayed discreetly where he was, glaring at Richard and rubbing a bumped head.

But Patty haughtily unfastened the ID bracelet from her wrist and flung it at Richard. "You can take this back, Mr. Harrison. And you needn't come to the beach party Saturday. Nobody cares whether you do or not!"

Richard snorted. "I don't need your invitation, Miss Lane. I've got other friends in the crowd. And anyhow, I'll be there on lifeguard duty. So, don't fall into the ocean or you might have to drag your own self out!" Then he wheeled and stamped back to the purple jalopy and climbed in.

Patty stared after him angrily, a bit stunned. She was suddenly tempted to run after him and tell him she was sorry for what she had said, but by now Byron was on his feet beside her, and she just stood staring bleakly.

Perhaps because Richard was so angry with Patty and Byron and the absent Cathy, he managed to kill his motor when he tried to start it. Annoyed, he made a second try, only to have the motor give a few feeble coughs and then expire.

Byron hooted mockingly and Richard seemed tempted to climb out of the car and come back to take it up with him.

"Better quit that or he'll come back!" Patty advised coldly.

"Aagh!" Byron said defiantly, but he stopped hooting.

A moment later, Richard had started the car and was backing it rapidly down the driveway. He took the curve into the street on two screeching wheels and disappeared.

Byron sneered, "What a drip! Strictly from nowhere!"

Patty turned on him furiously and slapped his face. Then she ran toward the house in tears.

Byron glared a moment and then stalked rapidly after her, holding his jaw and scowling.

He caught up with her in the hallway outside the library. He swung her around roughly by the arm and backed her violently against the wall.

"Apologize!" he demanded angrily.

"I'll yell if you don't let me go!" Patty threatened, trying to break free. Her eyes were flashing and her pretty face was flushed with anger.

But Byron only laughed, and then quite suddenly kissed her. A moment later he was very sorry for it. Patty had kicked him in the shin—hard.

Byron let go of her and yelled with pain. He began hopping around, holding his leg, and shouting, "You stupid little dame! Wait'll I—"

But Patty didn't hear any more. She had fled into the library and slammed the door behind her.

Byron started to follow, but his mother's voice stopped him. It was cold and hard. "Byron! I wish to speak to you in my room."

She was wearing her hat and gloves and had evidently just returned from some errand.

"OK, Mom," Byron said sulkily and followed her to her room, limping.

"What's on your mind?" Byron asked, throwing himself into the softest chair at hand. "I was just getting some kicks."

"Forget the nonsense. I have news for you. I've just come from Mr. Larch's office. Councilman Thad Brown was there. He tells me that that museum idea of Martin Lane's is to be voted on this coming week, before they adjourn until fall."

Byron looked alarmed. "Kind of rushing it, aren't they? Somebody must feel pretty sure about it, one way or the other."

His mother nodded grimly. "The majority are very much for it. In fact they are all coming here tomorrow night to look over the place and listen to Martin Lane's plans."

"Looks like curtains for Grammand and Larch's deal," Byron said glumly. "We could have had a ball with that commission."

"We still may. There's a chance!" Mira was smug.

"Planning to put arsenic in their punch tomorrow night?" Byron asked with a snicker. "Or to sic Jessie Belle's ghost on 'em and scare 'em off?"

"Strange you should have mentioned her. She's the very one I had in mind to help us."

Byron looked incredulous. "Hey, I hope you're not getting teched in the head about her like the old boy is!" He scoffed.

"What do *you* think, dear?" Mira asked coolly. "Am I the type?"

And as Byron listened to what his mother had in mind, he had to admit it was quite an idea, if they could put it over.

10 *A Trunkful of Treasures*

Down in the library, Cathy was feeling guilty as she listened to Patty's account of the quarrel between the two boys. "I'm sorry I told Richard to come," she told Patty. "I really wanted to help."

"Forget it!" Patty told her cheerfully. "It was fun!" She draped herself against the mantel, aping a bored debutante, and drawled, "Re-ahlly, my deah, it bolsters one's ego to be fought for!"

Cathy laughed, but sobered quickly. "I wish you'd make up with Richard before the beach party. He's so much nicer than Byron."

"Pooh for Byron! He's just a silly clown," Patty said loftily. Then she giggled. "But kinda cute, at that. I must tell Yvonne what he called Richard's precious new car!"

"I really don't think you should," Cathy advised.

Patty frowned. "Why not? It's just what he said, a relic!"

"But it might hurt Richard's feelings to think you made fun of it, when it's the best he can do for a car," Cathy explained gently.

Patty thought it over a moment. Then she sighed. "As usual, you're right. No use rubbing it in. Besides, I just might want to get that ID bracelet back one of these days. My wrist feels cold without it."

Mr. Trevett came bouncing in gaily just then, and Patty soon forgot her boy problems. He had a wonderful inspiration. He asked them to be junior hostesses and greet the councilmen and their wives at the reception.

"Maybe we should be wearing Colonial costumes and wigs and stuff! Wouldn't that be keen?" Patty suggested.

"Delightful idea!" Mr. Trevett beamed.

"We can hire gowns at the costumers—" Patty went on.

"Hire?" Mr. Trevett interrupted. "Nonsense! I imagine there's everything you'd need up in the attic. Trunksful. My dear wife and I saw them one day when we went exploring up there years ago. No one's been there since, so I'm quite sure —except for dust—they're still intact."

"We don't mind dust!" Patty exclaimed. "Come along, Cathy! I adore digging into old trunks. I'm a natural-born snooper like my dear little brother."

In a few minutes they started out, armed with a flashlight in case there were dark corners they wished to explore up in the attic.

They had passed Mira's door and were halfway up the stairs to the floor above, when they heard the door opening. They scurried up to the landing and crouched out of sight as Mira and her son emerged from the room and walked along the hall toward the descending stairs.

Mira's voice came distinctly to them. "I shall tell Dr. Stanton that these hallucinations seem to be increasing—" The rest of her words were lost as she and Byron descended to the lower floor.

The two girls looked at each other, puzzled. "What do you suppose is biting her?" Patty asked in a whisper.

"Maybe she's having nightmares," Cathy suggested. "Who's Dr. Stanton? Does your family go to him?"

"Goodness, no!" Patty said positively. "We have Dr. Davis, when we need a doctor. Stanton is probably a swanky specialist she's dug up somewhere."

"And costing poor Mr. Trevett plenty of money, I should imagine," Cathy guessed.

They went on up to the top floor. The door to the portrait gallery was closed now, and neither of them had any desire to go in there.

"Too spooky for me," Patty admitted.

The stairs to the attic were inside a small room at the rear. It had probably served as a bedroom for one of the many servants they must have had years ago. Now the room was empty except for a couple of pieces of wooden furniture, which Cathy ooh'd and ah'd over, showing Patty how it was put together without nails. It was undoubtedly a couple of hundred years old, she said, and real authentic Dutch. But Patty thought it was awful and went on toward the steep attic stairs, eager to explore.

Dust lay on everything, and Patty began to sneeze almost at once. Dust always did that to her, except when it was in her own room. Then it could stay, without causing her any distress, until her mother descended upon her with a dustcloth and put her to work.

"I bet the attic's even worse than this," she complained indignantly, between sneezes.

Cathy giggled at her wiggling nose and reached for the stair rail. Then she gasped and backed off. "Someone's been on these stairs recently," she whispered. "Footprints!"

"Somebody may be up there right now!" Patty whispered. "Could be tramps or something. You remember Ross and his friend Davey got in and wandered all around and nobody knew it. Others could do it, too. Let's go back down, but quick!" And she turned toward the door. "We'll tell—"

But Cathy stopped her. "Wait, look at the footprints. Whoever made them came down again. See, the 'down' ones are on top of the 'up' ones. So there's no one up there now, I'm sure."

"I'm glad *you're* sure, but I still think I'd rather

hire a costume," Patty said grimly.

"Very well, I shall go alone." Cathy put one foot on the stairs. "Give my regards to Jessie Belle's ghost if you see her." She went on up toward the attic door.

"Hey, wait for me!" Patty followed her up quickly. "No fair leaving me."

The attic was big and—except for neatly piled boxes, barrels, and discarded antique furniture in wrappings—it was empty. One small, ancient, leather-bound trunk had been drawn away from the others. It stood near a dormer window with an open shutter.

"That must be the one the Trevetts looked into," Patty said in a whisper. It seemed wrong to speak out loud.

Cathy nodded. She ran her hand over the leather, still in good condition and beautifully carved and trimmed. "It's a darling. I'm not sure, but I think it must have come from Spain in one of their trading ships. Shall we open it?"

"If you don't, I'm going to expire right now on this dusty floor!" Patty threatened.

Cathy lifted the heavy lid and looked in. Silks and satins, laces and ribbons, stiff brocade and gossamer sheer linens—all were jumbled as if someone had made a search for something, then had carelessly crammed the lovely things back into the old trunk.

Both girls exclaimed indignantly at sight of the tangle.

"It *must* have been tramps to treat these lovely things like this," Cathy moaned, smoothing them out lovingly.

But Patty had found a satin gown that was just her size, and she was holding it up against her. "Look, Cath! All it needs is ironing! And there's another one, blue velvet to go with this blue satin. Try it!"

It was perfect—or it would be after it was ironed—and Cathy loved every bit of real lace that trimmed its softly draped bodice.

They found a pair of satin slippers, but when they tried to put them on, they found that the lady who had worn them must have had a very small foot.

"I guess feet have changed," Patty commented a bit ruefully. "Remember how tiny Jessie Belle's feet looked in that painting of her."

"You know, maybe the things in this trunk were hers!" Cathy said breathlessly.

"It could be." Patty agreed with a shiver and an uneasy glance around the shadowy attic. "Here, put 'em back."

Cathy wrapped the slippers in their velvet case and tied it with the faded blue ribbon that almost fell apart as she fastened it. Then she tucked the package into a corner of the trunk and closed the lid on it.

"Let's take the loot and go. It's spooky!" Patty started for the door, carrying the two gowns.

But Cathy stooped and picked up another velvet shoecase from the floor beside the trunk. It was empty and the ribbon ties were ripped loose. The slippers it must have contained were not in sight, though Cathy flashed her light all around close to the trunk. Finally she dropped the case on the trunk and followed Patty. Probably the persons who had looted the trunk had found

Jessie Belle's gold slippers and intended to sell
them, if they could, Cathy thought.

They found Owen Trevett pacing the floor trying to memorize a speech. Martin Lane had sent
it over by messenger a short while before. It was
to follow Martin's own speech, after the council
had made their tour and were relaxing with refreshments. It was a short speech, but the old
gentleman was no speaker, and he was having
difficulty.

They showed him the gowns, and he tried to be
interested, but when Patty began, "And we found
something else interesting—" he stopped her, not
unkindly.

"Please, girls, I'm having a bit of trouble with
this speech dear Martin has written for me.
Would you take the pretty gowns and run along
home now? I'm most grateful for all your help,
and I'll look for you at an early hour tomorrow
afternoon to help me receive our guests."

"We'll be here good and early," Patty promised,
"all prettied up."

And they hurried away.

Patty chattered most of the way home, but Cathy was rather silent. Then, as they turned in at the house, Patty noticed the silence. "What now, fair lady?"

"I suppose it really doesn't matter, but I wish we had been able to tell him about people having been in the attic!"

"Seems to me he has enough on his mind, learning that speech," Patty observed wisely. "Besides, what good would it do to worry him about it, when the thieves are probably miles away now, trying to get a nickel or a dime for whatever they stole? And not having much luck, I imagine."

"I suppose you're right. We'll wait till after the party to tell him. Maybe when we bring back the gowns," Cathy conceded.

There wasn't much alteration necessary on the gowns, and both girls helped Natalie fix them. And the next afternoon the two girls were Colonial visions in satin and velvet—even to hired wigs, silvered and powdered.

They had practiced curtsies at great length, much to Ross's open amusement. Every time

Patty started to curtsy, Ross would pop his head around the doorjamb and pretend to be convulsed with laughter. Finally, she had had enough. She picked up her skirts and dashed at him. "Wait'll I get you, you monster!"

But Ross ducked again, and as Patty went through the doorway, he put out his foot and tripped her. She shrieked and started to tumble. But Martin was passing by and he caught her safely, though her wig fell over her face. Her father put his arms around her to restrain her from resuming the chase. "Whoa, there! Who's this? Jo-Jo the Dog-faced Boy?" He lifted the wig and peered under it inquiringly.

Patty stopped struggling and started to laugh as she pushed the wig from her face. Then she stopped laughing and glared at Ross. "Let me at him, Dad. Just this once. Please!"

Ross made a face and then darted away.

Natalie drew Patty back into the room with Cathy. She placed the two girls together. "Aren't they dolls?" she asked her husband. And he had to agree.

It was a few minutes later, as Martin drove
them up to the Trevett driveway, that they saw
Mira Burton and a distinguished-looking gray-
haired man arriving in the Duesenberg. Byron
was at the wheel.

They waited for the car to sweep in past them,
and Patty lifted her hand to wave. But neither
Mira nor her son gave any sign of recognition.

"I guess now I won't have to speak to him
tonight," Patty said. "That's a load off my mind."

"And mine!" Cathy added strongly as they
went on up the driveway, tottering a little on high
heels and holding their heavy skirts clear of the
pavement.

11   *The Vanishing Slipper*

The girls expected Byron to be lurking about as they came into the house, but there was no sign of him.

"Good!" Patty said belligerently. "One crack from him about our costumes, and I'd have flattened him."

Cathy giggled. "Maybe he's going to wear a costume, too."

"That I would like to see!" Patty grinned. "Satin pants on those legs would be a riot!"

They were still smiling about it as they approached the library door. The door was open and they could hear a man's deep voice speaking.

"My dear Mr. Trevett," it said soothingly, "this is a most unusual experience you say you had last night."

"I don't *say* so, Dr. Stanton. I *had* it! I saw Jessie Belle's poor little ghost outside my window just as plainly as I'm seeing you right now."

The girls looked at each other, startled. Cathy tried to pull Patty away, whispering, "We're not supposed to listen to private conversations." But Patty brushed off her hand and moved a step closer so she could hear everything. And after a moment's hesitation, Cathy listened, too.

"I keep telling dear Uncle Owen that he simply must have dreamed he saw something, but he persists in this—uh—mistake." Mira's voice whined.

"Of course, I do! I know what I saw! Something woke me, and I saw her staring in at me. When I started toward the window, she floated away. But it was Jessie Belle, all right."

In the hall, Patty whispered to Cathy, "Sounds to me like another of Byron's tricks. Maybe he thought Mr. Trevett would have a heart attack if he scared him, and he and his mother could inherit everything."

"Oh, Patty!" Cathy said reproachfully, suppressing a smile. "You read too many mystery stories!"

Patty tiptoed closer and applied her eye to the

crack of the door, keeping out of view of those inside the library. Then she turned to Cathy and whispered, "I don't like that doctor. He's looking at Mr. Trevett as if he thought he was crazy or something. Look!"

Cathy looked, and nodded grimly. "I imagine that he does," she whispered, drawing Patty away from the door with her, "and Mrs. Burton evidently thinks so, too."

"Really?" Patty was startled. "Why do you believe that?"

"Because yesterday, up in the hall, when she was talking about hallucinations and we thought she meant she'd been dreaming or something, she must have been worrying about Mr. Trevett and not herself."

"You mean," Patty gasped, "that Mr. Trevett may have been 'seeing' other things, too, that we don't know about?"

"It sounds that way," Cathy agreed gravely.

"And this Dr. What's-his-name is probably a psy— a psychiatrist?" Patty had a little difficulty with the word.

"I should think so." Cathy nodded. "Poor dear Mr. Trevett!"

"It's this spooky house," Patty said.

"Well, he'll soon be rid of it. Uncle Martin says there's practically no opposition to the museum except from that councilman named Brown, and he's sure Mr. Brown won't hold out after he has a good look around at all the city will be getting for a modest price."

Patty looked back toward the library door. She could still hear voices indistinctly. "Looks as if they're not leaving for awhile. Let's go watch the catering people set up the tables in the ballroom. We can come back later."

So they went up the grand staircase and into the ballroom that was being used for the first time in a generation. Stacks of chairs stood against the wall, and half a dozen efficient men and women were bustling about preparing long tables for the food and refreshments that were to be served after the guests had made their inspection of the mansion.

Down in the library, Mira was saying sooth-

ingly to Owen Trevett, "I think you're just tired out, Uncle, dear. You need a rest, and Dr. Stanton has a lovely place for that."

Mr. Trevett snorted impolitely. "I'm all right."

"Of course, you are, sir," Dr. Stanton assured him smoothly. "But a little rest in a quiet spot would be good for you. I'd like to recommend a week or so at—"

"Sorry, Doctor, but I'm not interested!" The little old man was becoming annoyed.

Mira drew herself up stiffly. "You should be, Uncle Owen. If you're not careful you'll have a nervous breakdown! All this hullabaloo about turning your home into a museum has been a terrible strain. You should forget that ridiculous idea!"

"Ho-ho!" The old man pointed an accusing finger at Mira. "So that's what is really bothering you! I might have known it! You're a stubborn woman, Mira, but I'm stubborn, too. You're not going to get me to give up my plans." He turned to Dr. Stanton. "Nervous breakdown, indeed! Pay no attention to her, Doctor." He chuckled.

"I have no doubt that your rest home would be a splendid place for someone to go who needed a rest, but I assure you that someone is not myself!" He stuck his jaw out and glared belligerently at Dr. Stanton.

"Please, Mr. Trevett, you must not excite yourself," Dr. Stanton warned him soothingly.

"And you needn't take that tone to me, sir!" Mr. Trevett snapped. "I'm not in my second childhood yet!"

"Uncle Owen! I have never been so humiliated!" Mira jumped to her feet abruptly, dabbing a handkerchief at her eyes and sniffling. "Come, Dr. Stanton! We don't have to stay here and be insulted." She swept toward the door.

"I'm sorry you feel as you do, Mr. Trevett," Dr. Stanton said stiffly, rising. "Mrs. Burton is a fine woman and she has your interests at heart. It is my opinion that you are definitely on the verge of a breakdown. Good day, sir!" He stalked out after Mira and closed the door.

Owen Trevett sat staring after them for a long time. He was uneasy now. There might be something to what Mira was saying. Perhaps he *was* getting overtired. He had been through a great deal, and he wasn't young any more. Last night had shaken him more, perhaps, than he had realized.

He sat, going over it in his mind, and found that he was still undecided. Maybe it *had* been Jessie Belle's ghost out there last night. Maybe not. But there was the matter of the gilded slipper. What was the answer to that?

Last night, after the face outside the window had drifted away, he had thought first of Byron and his silly tricks. The girls had told him how Byron had played "spook" to frighten them. He might have decided to plague his host with some illusion, just for "kicks".

He had hurried to the boy's room, hoping to catch him with evidence, and had found him apparently sound asleep and hard to awaken. Byron, finally awake, had been sarcastic and angry at being disturbed.

Mira had hurried in from her room, having heard their voices. When he had told her about the face at the window and his suspicion of Byron, she had scoffed. "Just a nightmare!" she had said, positive as usual. And when he had denied that, she had caustically suggested that it could be simple imagination, brought on by his being over-tired. "And also brought on," she had added, "by that silly story you told those Lane girls about Jessie Belle's mother and the figurehead downstairs!" She had laughed sarcastically. "If Jessie Belle is haunting tonight, I should think you'd find her down there, not floating around outside. Or don't ghosts mind the cool night air?"

He had stalked out after that and gone back to his room, but Mira's words had stayed in his mind. And along toward morning, still wide awake, hc had taken a flashlight and gone down to the figurehead room. He had felt a little foolish for doing it, and when he had flashed his light around and seen nothing unusual, he had started to leave again. It was then that he had seen the small, gilded slipper lying just inside the door at one side. He had overlooked it before because it was behind him as he used the flashlight. He picked it up, and found it strangely familiar.

Somewhere he had seen one like it.

Then he remembered. It was a Turkish slipper with a turned-up toe, decorated with paste jewels and gold braid. And it was exactly like the gay little slippers that Jessie Belle had worn when she posed for the portrait now hanging upstairs. Jessie Belle's slipper!

"Jessie Belle," he had called softly, "are you here now?" But there had been no answer, and after a few moments he had begun to feel foolish and had left with the slipper.

He had hurried upstairs and on impulse had stopped to knock on Mira's door. After several taps, she had answered sleepily and he had called through the door that he had found something downstairs that he wished to show her.

Mira had replied crossly that whatever it was it could wait till morning. She was quite comfortable where she was. "And please stop prowling about, Uncle Owen, dear. You could catch pneumonia."

He had stomped off to his room after that and laid the gilded slipper on his night stand, where he would be able to see it first thing in the morning.

But when he had awakened in broad daylight, the slipper had disappeared.

When he had told Mira and Byron about it this morning, they had both looked surprised and exchanged peculiar looks. And when he had asked Mira just what those looks meant, she had waspishly told him that evidently he had been having another nightmare. He had snapped angrily at her and stalked out of the breakfast room. But Byron's words, "He's goofy, Mom!" had been audible even through the closed door.

And then, a few minutes ago, Mira had brought the stranger, this Dr. Stanton, to meet him. The fellow seemed pleasant enough, but it was evident at once that Mira had told him about the face at the window and the disappearance of the gold slipper. One didn't need to be very shrewd to guess that Dr. Stanton was making a professional visit and not a social one.

It had angered him so much that he had taken a firm stand—a lot firmer than he really felt—

declaring that he was positive that he had seen Jessie Belle's ghostly face outside the window. And while Mira made protesting sounds, he said grimly that he believed Jessie Belle had left him the gilded slipper as a sign and then had taken it away by some supernatural means.

Mira had reacted angrily—and revealed her real reason for calling in her doctor friend. He felt sure now that she had hoped to entice him into going away for a rest, so she could say he was too ill to negotiate with the council just then. The delay until fall would give her more time to work on him to sell to the apartment builders.

He thought a little sadly about the face he had seen at the window and the vanishing slipper, and though he disliked giving up the fantasy—it was like chopping off dear Jessie Belle's ghostly little head—he had to admit to himself that the goings-on last night had probably—no, *surely*—been Mira's and Byron's doings! All part of her trick to convince him that he did actually need a rest. But the trick had—what was Patty's favorite word—*flopped*.

He intended to tell Martin Lane all about last night's doings, but Martin arrived with half a dozen councilmen in tow and there was no chance for private conversation.

However, Mr. Trevett was in high spirits as he greeted his guests and their wives, and Martin wondered what he was chuckling about.

As soon as Patty and Cathy had made the ladies welcome and seen that they found their way to the powder rooms to leave their wraps, Martin called them aside.

"What's been going on around here? Mr. T. seems to be quite jubilant over something."

Patty looked at Cathy, and Cathy raised her eyebrows and nodded. "I guess we have to confess," Patty began hesitantly.

"Out with it, girl!" Martin pretended to frown.

"Well, we accidentally snooped—and we heard—" She looked appealingly to her cousin and gulped. "You tell Dad."

"It can't be that bad! Mr. T. seems too happy!" Martin laughed.

"I'm afraid it isn't very good, Uncle Martin,"

Cathy said gravely. "Mr. Trevett saw Jessie Belle's ghost last night."

"No!" Martin chuckled. "He's just teasing you two!"

Both girls shook their heads. "He didn't tell us. We accidentally heard him tell Mrs. Burton and a doctor she brought to see him," Patty explained.

"And not five minutes ago Patty heard Mrs. Burton tell Councilman Brown's wife that Mr. Trevett really should have a guardian because he has hallucinations."

"And isn't responsible for anything he does," Patty added glumly. "And that catty Mrs. Brown said, 'Good!' "

But Martin Lane had heard enough. With a wild look in his eyes, he turned and dashed off to find Owen Trevett.

Martin found the inspection group gathered around Mr. Trevett in the room containing the figurehead. The old gentleman was telling, with great gusto, the story of the lost "Jessie Belle" and the sad sequel of the bereaved mother who had come there to be close to her lost daughter's image.

"And even if Ahab's diary didn't exactly say so, I feel sure Jessie Belle's ghost must have come many a time to comfort her mother," Mr. Trevett finished.

Martin saw the looks that several of the councilmen exchanged, some wondering and some rather grim. Trevett wasn't doing the museum cause any good. And Martin noticed that Mira was keeping up a steady whisper to Councilman and Mrs. Brown behind her hand.

"Now, Mr. Trevett!" Brown said with a laugh.

"Don't tell us anybody in his right mind believes in ghosts!"

"And why not?" Trevett asked lightly. He shook a reproachful finger at the councilman and smiled a pixielike smile. "Think how many more admission tickets we could sell if we had a nice, pretty little ghost like Jessie Belle likely to show up any time without warning?"

Some of the councilmen laughed and clapped, but the ladies didn't look very happy, especially those who had been near enough to Mira to hear her whispers.

"I do hope your uncle isn't serious," Mrs. Brown whispered, loudly enough so the other ladies around them could hear.

"I'm afraid he is," Mira answered in the same tone. "In fact, he actually believes that he saw her last night!"

The ladies looked shocked and whispered among themselves, and their husbands murmured doubtfully to each other.

Martin looked grim. He would have to stop Trevett before he said any more. Next he would be telling them of his own experience with the ghost at the window. That would really convince them that he was off his rocker!

"If I may interrupt—" Martin pushed forward. "We forgot to mention that everything—furniture, paintings, the full collection of art objects that the Trevett mansion contains—everything is to be donated by Mr. Trevett to the museum without cost to the city!" He turned to Mr. Trevett. "Is that right, sir?"

"Indeed it is!" Mr. Trevett assured him.

There was a genuine outburst of applause and approving comment from most of the councilmen. Then at Martin's suggestion the party moved out of the room to ascend the grand staircase and inspect the rest of the house.

But Martin signaled Mr. Trevett that he wished to speak to him, and the old gentleman turned the tour over to Mira— "just for a few minutes, my dear, if you don't mind"—and she quickly took command, glad of the chance.

"And now, my boy, what is on your mind?" Trevett asked when they were alone.

Martin told him what the girls had heard Mira telling Mrs. Councilman Brown. "I don't like the sound of it. You realize, of course, that if there were any suspicion that you were—uh—unbalanced, any agreement you might sign regarding the property would be subject to challenge in court."

Mr. Trevett looked shocked. "But who would think such a ridiculous thing?"

"For one, Thad Brown. And he has a couple more votes on his side. He's helped that building firm on several big apartment house deals. He'll keep plugging away at this ghost thing." Martin hardly knew what to say without risking offending the old fellow. If Trevett really did believe he had seen Jessie Belle's ghost last night, he would resent questioning. But Martin had to know. "I understand that you saw—" He paused lamely. "That is, she—"

To his surprise, Mr. Trevett stopped him, chuckling and holding up his hand. "No, I didn't see Jessie Belle last night. It was a fake. I know that. I wanted very much to believe it had been real. It would have meant a great deal to me. But I decided that it was only a trick of Mira's to make me think that I am about to have a nervous breakdown. She wanted me to go to a rest home and let her do my thinking for me—especially, I'm sure, about selling this place to the city. She was still harping on that apartment house offer. But I've stopped her."

"Then why—that is, you seemed to believe just now—"

"I was joking, of course! I'm sure everyone understood that!" He was indignant. "People like to be scared."

"I'm afraid they took you seriously, with Mira's help," Martin said gravely.

"Then I shall make a point of telling them all at supper that I was merely having a little fun. And I'll clip Mira's claws by turning the laugh on her and her precious son by telling the trick they tried to play on me last night." Trevett waved it aside lightly.

But Martin shook his head and looked glum. "I don't think that will help much. They may choose to believe Mira's version." He frowned thoughtfully. Then his face brightened. "Wait a minute! I think we can convince them you were joking, but we'll need Patty's or Cathy's help!"

The girls were watching the last stragglers go up the broad staircase. They had offered to help Mira show the visitors around and had been royally snubbed.

Martin came striding up to them. "You'll be happy to learn that Mr. Trevett wasn't serious about seeing Jessie Belle's ghost, after all," he told them.

"Thank heaven!" Patty rolled her eyes.

When he told them what he was planning, they both eagerly agreed to do their best to put it over.

A few minutes later, they stole up the back stairway without encountering anyone on the way. They were particularly careful as they drew near the floor on which were Byron's and his mother's rooms.

"Of all people we don't want to meet just now, Byron is the most." Patty giggled.

The gallery was handsomely lit with tall candles and all the dust covers were piled in the storage closet at the far end of the hall. The gilded antique chairs gleamed in the flickering candlelight, but there were deep shadows around the door of the storage closet. The girls disappeared into the closet just a few seconds before the inspection party came noisily up the final flight of stairs.

"Here they come now," Patty whispered excitedly as Mr. Trevett and Mira led the group in and started to take them for a tour of the ancestral portraits in their gilded frames.

There were admiring expressions and exclamations of excitement as Mr. Trevett paused before one life-size painting.

"And this is Jessie Belle," he told them loudly. "Perhaps if we are very quiet, we might be honored by a sight of her. Hush now, everybody."

Some of the ladies tittered but Councilman Brown said distinctly, "More silly stuff!"

Mr. Trevett turned to him reproachfully shaking his head. "Please, Mr. Brown! You'll hurt her feelings. Please be quiet for a moment."

"Rot! I'm getting out of this spooky—" He stopped abruptly and stared at something at the far end of the long gallery.

Mr. Trevett wheeled and stared, too. And several feminine shrieks broke the silence.

A figure swathed in long white draperies was advancing out of what seemed the dark wall—but was really the door—of the storage room.

"Jessie Belle," Mr. Trevett said softly but distinctly enough to be sure all his guests heard it.

The figure continued to advance, almost as if it were floating. Candlelight flickered on it and the startled spectators could see that a piece of drapery covered its face.

As one, they retreated from it step by step. The figure began waving its arms gracefully and making moaning noises. From somewhere came the faint sound of a harmonica, favorite of the old-time seamen as they gathered in the forecastle. The tune was the old sea chantey, "Blow the Man Down."

It was very convincing, and Patty, under the draperies, was having a ball. She decided to add a few twists and twirls for good measure—and bumped into a spindly chair.

Down went the chair and down went Patty with a shriek. There was a confused flurry of dustcover draperies, and then Patty sat nursing a knee, her wig over one ear as she wailed, "Ouch, that hurt!"

Tension snapped and almost everyone surged forward laughingly to see who the fake ghost was. Mira and the Browns exchanged baffled looks and held back. Mira scowled as Martin called out, "Patty, you little fake!" and ran to help her to her feet.

Mr. Trevett chuckled. "That last part wasn't in the act, ladies and gentlemen, but you'll have to admit it was a great finish!" Then he called out, "Come on, Ghost Number Two!" And Cathy marched out in her dustcover draperies, playing a rather garbled version of "Yankee Doodle."

It brought a small cheer and then President Peterson slapped Mr. Trevett on the back. "So all the buildup about ghosts was a joke, you rascal! You had us all going for awhile, didn't he, folks?"

There were laughing agreements in reply and then at the host's suggestion, they all trooped down to dinner. Except Mira Burton. She started toward the ballroom with the others, but at her own floor she quietly slipped away and entered her own room.

Patty, the only one who seemed to notice her leaving, confided mischievously to Cathy, "I don't think Mrs. B. liked our performance. My feelings are hurt!"

"Mine, too!" Cathy said with a twinkle. "I imagine she's gone to cry on dear Byron's shoulder because their little plot failed."

"I bet Byron shows up for the eats, just the same." Patty laughed. "And that's when I'm going to inform him that the beach party is called off tomorrow. We don't want him."

"But you can't do that!" Cathy protested.

"Oh, can't I? I invited him," Patty said grimly, "and I can *dis*invite him!"

"I doubt if he'll even consider coming, after getting slapped and kicked!"

"He'd better not," Patty said fiercely.

Byron slouched on the satin-covered sofa and eyed his mother gloomily. "Looks as if the old boy outfoxed you, Mom. All that talk he did in front of Dr. Stanton was phony. He must have seen you sneak in and get that slipper when you thought he was asleep."

Mira shook her head. "No, he was snoring hard. And I'm sure he *did* believe he'd seen Jessie Belle's ghost. Dr. Stanton thinks so, too. He thinks dear Uncle Owen should spend a few days—or weeks, maybe—under competent observation. Dr. Stanton thinks he might become violent unless he has proper care."

Byron snickered. "What about that switch he did, upstairs tonight—getting the Lane girls to clown as ghosts? Doesn't that sort of upset the idea that he's goofy?"

"It might," she said serenely, "but only until the council learns that he has had to be put into a rest home after a violent outburst that took place after all the guests had gone home. I've already phoned Dr. Stanton to report it. He's sending two attendants to pick up dear Uncle Owen tomorrow."

"The old boy will have something to say about that," Byron predicted. "How you going to handle it?"

Myra picked up a bottle of pills from her bedside table and rattled them. "Uncle Owen will be asleep. The servants are off tomorrow. And you'll be at the beach with the Lane girls." She slipped the bottle into her pocket. "And now, after the others leave, I shall tuck Uncle Owen into bed and see that he takes his glass of hot milk."

13 *Beach Party*

"What time is Richard calling for you girls?" Natalie asked as she packed their lunch basket the next morning.

"He isn't," Patty said flatly.

"Don't tell me you two haven't made up your squabble yet!" Natalie was surprised.

"Oh, we're definitely through," Patty told her mother casually. Much too casually for a young lady who had been hopefully racing to answer the phone every time it had rung that early morning.

"That's too bad," Natalie said cheerfully. "Then how do you expect to get to the beach party?"

"Cathy and I sort of thought you and Dad might drop us off, long as he doesn't have to go to the office today."

"I'm afraid not, dear. Our day is already

planned. You had better phone Yvonne and see if she and Earl can squeeze you into that old wreck of Earl's somehow."

"But, Mom! They'll have their surfboards and Earl's skin-diving junk and food and— There won't be room."

"Then call one of your other friends!"

"They're all filled up. We were counting on you."

"I'm sorry. Dad has to see the antique car parade. J. R. is going to have his 'thirty-seven Mercedes-Benz in it, and he expects Dad to lead the cheering for it—or be in the doghouse."

"Well, OK, Mom. But it's a moth-eaten drag. Earl is so persnickety about that heap. A scratch on it is a mortal wound!"

It *was* a bit crowded in Earl's car, but Yvonne persuaded Earl to take them. He had a last word, however, before they pulled away, loaded down with paraphernalia from the Lane residence: "And keep your hands off the chrome, huh?"

They both promised to be super-careful, but Patty grew tired of being poked in the neck by the edge of a balsa-wood surfboard. She was surprised after they had gone only a few blocks to hear the familiar Duesenberg roar coming along behind them. She peeked out from under a load of gear and lunch baskets, beach mats and beach hats.

"It's Byron in the Duesy!" she informed Cathy. "Of all the nerve!" She shoved the surfboard away in exasperation. Then she grinned at Cathy. "Well, since he's here—" she said. Then she called out, "Hi, Byron! Going our way?" as the big car roared up close beside Earl's.

"Hey! Watch it, fella!" Earl yelled and swerved, almost hitting the curb. The girls screamed.

Byron laughed and maneuvered the big car so that it partially blocked the path of the smaller one. Earl had to stop. Byron called, "How about riding in a real car, Patty? Cathy?"

Earl started to unwind himself from behind the wheel. "Get that oversized clunker out of the way, Bud, or I'll paste you!"

"It's all right, Earl!" Patty scrambled out from under the load.

"Coming, kids?" Byron looked down from his lofty seat.

"Sure!" Patty scrambled all the way out of the car. "Come on, Cathy!"

"I'll be fine here, thanks," Cathy told her. But Patty grabbed her wrist and pulled, and Cathy had to get out.

"See you later," Patty told Yvonne as they transferred their lunch basket and other junk, and climbed in beside Byron.

They were scarcely settled when Byron gunned his motor and roared off with a screech of tires.

"Wonder where they met that showboat?" Earl said disgustedly. "He comes on like a windmill in a hurricane!"

"Doesn't he?" Yvonne agreed, but she looked wistful. It was a groovy car. And Byron was sophisticated looking. But Earl was awfully sweet about helping her with math. A girl couldn't ask for everything!

From his lookout post above the stretch of beach, Richard stared glumly out to sea. The usual bevy of girls had spread their beach mats close enough to his post for him to notice their new bathing suits if he wished to, but Richard was thinking of Patty, and he had a single-track mind.

He had tried several times to phone her last night, but got a busy signal each time. Finally he had decided to wait till today and try the personal touch. He hoped she was ready to make up.

Almost all the group had arrived. Some were playing touch tag, others were trying the surf, and others were just lolling under their umbrellas. But Patty was still missing. Maybe she wasn't coming.

Richard noticed several of the kids animatedly watching something back at the parking strip. The tag game had stopped, and the players were watching excitedly, too. Richard looked—and he wished he hadn't. Patty and Cathy were arriving in style—in that same Duesenberg she had been helping to polish at the Trevett mansion. And the driver was Byron Burton.

Richard turned his back to them quickly and

stared out at the ocean with noticeable attention
to duty. He yelped at a couple of youngsters who
were venturing out toward the riptide flow and
sternly ordered them to the beach out of danger.

Patty chose the spot where she and Cathy and
Byron would settle with their paraphernalia. It
was close to the lifeguard post but Patty made a
point of not looking that way.

Byron lolled under the umbrella, but Patty
greeted her friends loudly and cheerfully, chal-
lenged the gang to start another game of touch
tag, and in general made herself conspicuous.
Cathy settled down with a magazine.

Richard looked the other way as the game went
on noisily with girls shrieking and darting about,
and boys yelling and chasing them. Patty was the
noisiest. She seemed to be having a wonderful
time.

Byron smoked and lolled on his beach mat,
cynically watching the game but declining Patty's
attempt to coax him to join it. Finally he leaned
over, plucked Cathy's magazine from her hands,
and said, "This is a washout. Let's cut out on

these infants. We'll find a jukebox where we can dance."

"No, thanks," Cathy said coldly. "I prefer to stay here. But don't let me stop you. Run right along. Patty and I won't mind a bit." And with that, before he could think up something sarcastic to say, she was on her feet and running lightly down the beach to the water.

Byron scowled after her, tempted to follow. Then he noticed that the tag game had broken up and Patty was heading for the umbrella, staggering and breathless. He waited.

She flopped down on her towel. "Boy, that was fun! I'm beat!" But she sat up again quickly as a clap of thunder sounded. She looked up at the sky, startled. Heavy clouds were moving in. A storm was about to break. "Darn! It *would* rain today!" she complained. Then she missed Cathy. "Hey, where's Cathy?"

Byron pointed to a swimmer out beyond the breakers. "She's quite a swimmer."

"She should have waited for me. It's silly to swim alone," Patty said.

Byron laughed. "She won't be lonesome." He nodded toward Richard's post. "She's no dope."

Patty saw that Richard's lookout post was empty and Richard was striding down to the surf. A moment later he was swimming strongly out toward Cathy.

"Cousin Cathy seems to have scored with your boyfriend," Byron laughed. "Right under your little nose!"

"Pooh! Who cares?" Patty shrugged and looked away.

A flash of lightning and an immediate loud clap of thunder brought shrieks from the girls and a general scramble to get under the wooden pier as the rain started pelting down.

Patty glanced toward the water. Richard and Cathy were swimming in now, side by side. When they reached shallower water Cathy seemed to stumble as they stood up, waist high, and Richard put his arm around her to steady her. Patty felt sick suddenly.

Byron saw her expression. He took her arm. "Let's scram. The guy's a chiseler. What do you want to moon around about him for?"

"I'm not!" Patty almost shouted.

"Oh, yeah?" he gibed. "Well, stay here and cry. I'm going!" And he started away.

Patty took a deep breath and then tossed her head. "Let's go! Beat you to the car!" And she ran off, laughing back at Byron as if they were playing. Byron snatched up his sweater and dashed after her.

Richard had a strong grip on Cathy's arm as they came up from the water. She was staggering a little. He coaxed her, "Just a few feet more!" And then they were on dry sand.

Cathy said, "Thanks!" and looked up toward the umbrella for Patty. She and Richard saw them at the same time. They had just reached the big car.

"Patty! Wait!" Cathy called out, but a clap of thunder drowned her voice. And a moment later Byron and Patty were in the car and Byron was making the motor roar. Cathy and Richard watched helplessly as the big car pulled away fast from the parking strip, picked up speed, and hurtled away along the beach road.

Earl had come up. "That guy's asking for trouble driving like that on a wet road! Patty's out of her mind to ride with him."

"She sure is," Richard agreed gravely. Then his anger flashed. "If she gets hurt, I'll personally—" He stopped. He couldn't think of anything bad enough. "I'm going after them. I haven't got the speed, but traffic's bound to slow him down soon. Will you take over my job till I get back?"

"Sure thing! Hope you overhaul him before he crashes it!"

Richard started to stride away toward his jalopy. Cathy ran after him. "I'm going with you!"

The beach road was slick with rain and once Byron was out of sight of the beach party, he slowed down a trifle. Patty was relieved. She had been more than slightly worried.

"I think I'd like to go home," Patty said, meekly for her.

"OK," Byron said indifferently. "Drop you off."

He drove on a few blocks before he became

aware that the purple jalopy, with Richard at the wheel and Cathy beside him, was pursuing them. Richard was signaling by blinking his lights. They flashed in the rearview mirror. Patty, who hadn't noticed, was staring off gloomily. Byron stepped on the accelerator and the big car began to roll fast.

Patty was jolted. She screamed. "Don't go so fast!" she called, hanging onto the door. "You'll hit something!" He took a corner on two wheels, skidded wildly, righted the car in time to avoid hitting a telephone pole, and drove on. When he looked back, the other car was out of sight.

But a little sports car was speeding toward him in the rain. The driver was practically on the divider line. So was Byron.

"Pull over! You'll hit him!" Patty yelled and grabbed at the wheel. But Byron struck her hand aside.

"Watch him chicken out!" he shouted and drove on.

The sports car failed to give ground. It came straight ahead.

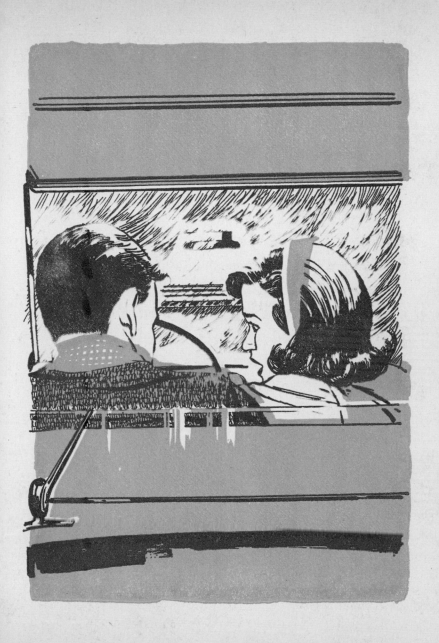

And at the very last second, it was Byron who panicked. He wrenched the big car's wheel over hard and the sports car whipped past with only inches to spare. It vanished into the murky rain with an insolent blast of its horn.

But Byron had turned his wheels too far. The Duesenberg went up over the curb, across the shoulder, and into a rock-strewn open field. Fright had frozen Byron's hands to the wheel and all he could do was sit there clutching it, while the car headed straight for a cluster of big boulders.

Patty screamed a warning, but Byron was beyond heeding. She leaned over quickly and turned the ignition key.

She was barely in time to avoid a nasty smash-up. The heavy car hit the rocks—but not hard enough to be wrecked. The jolt knocked Byron free of the wheel and his head hit the heavy wooden bar that supported the car top. He slid to the floor behind the wheel in an unconscious heap.

Patty was badly shaken but not injured. She had dropped to the floor at the last second, shielding her head with her arms. She scrambled up into her seat again and saw Byron on the floor. She clutched his arm and tried to drag him up onto the seat, but he was too limp. Almost hysterical, she urged him, "Get up, Byron. Please get up!"

But he only groaned and pushed feebly at her hand. "Let me alone, Mom," he whined. "I'm sleepy." And he didn't lift his head.

"You must wake up! Please don't go to sleep!" She shook him, and he began mumbling incoherently. She listened, shocked.

"You said—you could—do it yourself—" he muttered. "Sleeping pills—old fool—give no—more trouble. . . ."

Patty leaned close. He was mumbling unintelligibly now. But she hadn't the least doubt but that he had been talking about Mr. Trevett! "Yes, Byron," she whispered encouragingly. "No—more—trouble—"

He began to mumble again. "Stanton—rest home—legal guardian—clever, Mom. . . ." After that all he did was groan and fumble for his head, where a sizable lump had formed.

Patty shivered. She thought she could guess what he might have been talking about. Mrs. Burton had tried to get poor old Mr. Trevett into Dr. Stanton's rest home. Now maybe she intended to do it with sleeping pills! And maybe pretend he was out of his mind! She'd tried it last night and failed!

14 *The Rescue Squad*

Patty was scared and worried. She felt like adding a second lump to the unconscious Byron's head as she realized what his mutterings might have meant. She could see that he was coming out of his daze now. Maybe he would remember what he had said and try to make her promise not to tell anyone. But she wouldn't promise. She'd tell her father the very minute she got home!

But would Byron take her home, if he knew? She was thoroughly frightened by now, and she decided not to stay in the car with Byron another minute. She climbed out as he was starting to pull himself back up, groaning, into the driver's seat.

Then she heard the other car—the purple jalopy—coming across the field. She was so relieved to see Richard and Cathy that she ran as fast as she could to meet them, stumbling and sloshing through the rain.

Cathy was out of the jalopy almost before Richard had braked to a stop. She ran to meet Patty. "Are you all right? Did that idiot wreck the car?"

"He did his best," Patty told her grimly, with an angry look back at Byron who was slowly climbing out of the Duesenberg holding his head. "Barney Oldfield the second! Or maybe his name is Benedict Arnold the second! It fits!"

"Whatever are you talking about?" Cathy was bewildered.

But Patty was watching Richard get out of his car and come toward them. She expected him to ask how she felt, and was all ready to collapse prettily on his arm. But Richard stalked grimly past her as if he didn't see her and headed for Byron. Patty glared after him angrily.

"Never mind. It doesn't matter," she told Cathy shortly. "Nobody cares what I think, anyhow. My own cousin steals my steady right under my nose—and—" Her voice broke and a single tear dropped.

"Patty!" Cathy shook her by the arm. "Stop that nonsense! I never heard of riptides and I was doing everything out there in the water that I shouldn't have done to get away from one of them. Richard saw me struggling and swam out and saved my life. And you— Oh!" She shook Patty hard.

"Oh, C-Cathy, I'm sorry!" And a moment later they were hugging each other tearfully.

Beside the big Duesenberg, Richard was making a quick inspection of Byron's bumped head and not looking too worried. Byron was scowling and sullen.

"I hope he has a headache for a week," Patty said, brushing away a last teardrop. "Wait till I tell you—" She repeated what Byron had muttered while he was dazed.

She had scarcely finished when Byron came roaring past, his big car splashing mud over both girls. He bumped over the rough ground to the road and disappeared toward town.

Richard sloshed up to them.

"Is Byron's head all right?" Cathy asked.

"As right as it will ever be without any brains in it!" he said. Then he added, "But some people like the type."

"Thank you, sir," Patty said stiffly.

"Don't mention it!" Richard snapped. Then he turned to Cathy. "Want to go back to the beach?"

"In th-this rain?" Cathy's teeth were chattering. Both she and Patty looked like drowned rats.

Richard found it hard to restrain himself from trying to put his arms around poor Patty and telling her how glad he was that she hadn't been hurt. But he steeled himself and said casually, "OK, hop in. I'll take you home. You both better get out of those wet things."

"G-Good," Cathy said, and herded Patty along after Richard as he stalked silently to his car. "Maybe we should ask Richard what we ought to do about Mr. Trevett," Cathy whispered.

"Indeed not!" Patty stuck out a stubborn chin. "We can think of something ourselves without any help from him!"

All the way home, Patty sat silent and aloof.

An awkward silence struck Cathy and Richard, too, after a feeble effort at polite conversation.

The rain had stopped when they reached the Lane home. Patty said stiffly, "Much obliged," as she got out of the jalopy. She swept into the house like a duchess.

Cathy lingered a moment to whisper to the grim-faced Richard, "She was acting up because she was jealous. You're still—what is Patty's word for it—*top cat?*" Then as Richard beamed in response, she hurried after Patty with a happier face. And Richard drove off, smiling broadly.

"I'm going to tell Dad what Byron said, right now!" Patty told Cathy. Then she remembered that her father and mother were out and would not be home perhaps for hours. The horseless carriage parade probably hadn't even started—or had been held back by the rain.

"Do you think I should go to the police station and tell them?" Patty asked uneasily.

"I don't know," Cathy admitted. "They might think you made it up because you'd had a quarrel with Byron or some sort of thing like that." She added gently, "It *is* pretty wild."

"But I heard him!" Patty said with a touch of anger.

"Even if they believed you, they might think he was joking, just to tease you."

"But he wasn't joking. He called me 'Mom' twice! And he didn't know what he was saying, I'm sure," Patty insisted. "Cathy, what are we going to do? We can't let them put Mr. Trevett in some horrible old 'rest home' with that stuffy Dr. Stanton in charge of him. He might never get out!"

"Why don't we go over there as soon as we change out of these wet things? We'll simply tell Mr. Trevett what you heard Byron talking about, and he can take it from there himself." Cathy was excited now.

"Super! We'll take along some of the museum letters from Dad's file and pretend they just came and that Dad wants Mr. Trevett to have them right away. She won't have any idea why we came and we'll tell Mr. Trevett the whole thing as soon as she leaves us alone with him."

They dashed about breathlessly changing their clothes and drying their hair. In less than half an hour they were on their way to the big mansion.

Soon the girls were hurrying in through the gates and up to the front door. Mira Burton answered the bell. She was surprised to see them but regained her composure at once. She held the door only partly open as she told them, "I'm sorry, girls, but my dear uncle cannot have any company today. He tired himself out with that silly party last night. His doctor says he must spend a day or so in bed till he is stronger. I know you will understand." She had almost closed the door.

"But these letters—Dad says—" Patty showed her the packet.

Mira promptly plucked the letters from Patty's hand. "I'll take them to him. Thank you." And she stepped back quickly, closing the door in their faces.

There seemed to be nothing they could do but return home.

"What do you think about that?" Patty asked angrily.

"I suppose he could really be tired," Cathy said, but she frowned uncertainly.

"Well, I think it shows there's something going on!"

"What can we do to find out?" Cathy asked helplessly. "Maybe we'd better just go home and wait till Uncle Martin gets there. He'll probably go right over and make her let him see Mr. Trevett."

"I guess that's the best way. Dad would be able to tell right away if there's anything going on."

But just as they were about to step out through the gates, they had to jump back into the shrubbery to avoid an unmarked white panel truck that was turning in at the driveway. It sped past them and up to the front of the mansion. The driver and a second man in a white jacket went up the steps, carrying something that looked very much like a stretcher to Patty and Cathy.

The girls watched from the shrubbery. As the front door was opened by Mira, they shrank back as far as they could, so she wouldn't see them. But she didn't look in their direction. She greeted the two men and beckoned them in. They went past her with the stretcher and she closed the door.

"They're going to take him away now! We won't have time to wait and tell Dad. We've got to get into that house somehow and try to help Mr. Trevett!" Patty wailed. "But how?"

"I could show you how to get in," Ross's voice said from somewhere deeper in the shrubbery. He poked his head out and grinned at them. "What's going on?"

"What are you doing here?" Patty demanded.

"Same thing as you. Snooping."

"Snooping for what?" Cathy asked.

"The gold slipper, so I can show it to Davey. It must be hidden somewhere in the house," Ross told her.

"And who told you about any gold slipper?" his sister asked threateningly.

He looked at her owlishly and snickered. "Bugged your room with my intercom last night," he confessed happily. "Heard you two gabbing about it. Bet I can find it."

"You little—ooh! You wait till I tell Mom what a little sneak—" Patty glared at him.

"Thought you were achin' to get into the house? *I* can! I could tell *how* but I won't now!" Ross said defiantly. "Find out for yourself." He started to leave the shrubbery. "I guess I'll trot on home now." And he headed toward the gate.

"Wait! If you'll tell us, you can borrow my tennis racket any time without asking," Patty promised hastily.

He looked at her doubtfully.

"And I'll be glad to teach you all about cricket," Cathy added.

Ross's face brightened. "You mean that?"

Cathy nodded. "First lesson tomorrow!"

"OK, then. I can trust *you* to keep your promise," he told Cathy, with a meaningful look at his sister. "Come on. We have to go through the rear fence. There's a busted pane in the basement window where you can reach in and unlock it."

They took one last careful look at the front

door of the mansion but saw no sign of anyone watching. Then all three darted out through the gate.

In the rear of the big house, they caught a glimpse of Byron at the garage, and heard him hammering on metal. He was probably trying to hammer out the dent in the front fender where it hit the rock.

They got through the coal-bin window safely, and started up the enclosed rear stairway that led to the upper stories. Only the servants used that stairway, and it was their day off.

They made as little noise as they could. And in a few minutes they reached the floor on which Mr. Trevett's suite was located. Everything seemed quite still up there, and the girls and Ross started toward the door of the suite. Then they heard voices on the floor below, and realized that Mrs. Burton was leading the men up the stairs. They darted into a hall closet and crouched there.

Mrs. Burton was saying, "My dear uncle insisted upon taking several sleeping pills last night, and he may still be asleep. He had hallucinations after that reception, and really became quite violent after his guests left." She was rattling a bunch of keys as she came to the landing. "I thought it was safer to lock him in."

"He'll be OK at Restful Haven, ma'am. Doc Stanton knows how to handle 'most any case."

"I certainly hope a rest will do my uncle a lot of good, but—" She was fitting the key into the lock now. It turned with a grating sound. "Right in here—" Mira began. Then she stopped suddenly. "He's gone!" she said unbelievingly. "But he can't be! I looked in on him not five minutes ago and he was sound asleep!"

"Looks as if he had another key," a gruff voice said.

"But the door was still locked just now!" Mira told him.

"Sometimes they're pretty cagey. Probably locked it so you wouldn't notice he was gone. Maybe he's still in there, though, hiding. Let's take a good look."

Their voices receded, and the girls heard sounds of a search. But soon they heard the three come out, planning a search of the house. Byron had joined them now, and he suggested that he and his mother would look upstairs in the portrait gallery. "Dear Uncle Owen" might have gone up there to commune with his favorite ghost.

So the men started a swift search on the lower floors while the Burtons went up to the gallery.

It was stuffy now in the hall closet, and the girls popped out the moment the hall was clear. Ross followed, dragging a length of filmy material attached to the mask of a girl's face. He had a small gilded slipper in his other hand.

"Look what I found bundled up in there!" he whispered excitedly. "Is this the ghost an' the slipper?"

"It must be!" Patty exclaimed in a stage whisper. "See that piece of string tied to the mask, and the silk is real thin. It would float sort of spooky, I bet. They probably dangled it outside the window from upstairs."

"Wonder why they didn't burn it up or get rid of it somehow," Cathy puzzled.

Patty had an answer. "Probably meant to later and then got cooking up this deal and overlooked it. We'd better hide it somewhere for evidence."

"Where would be the best place?" Ross asked.

"In Mr. Trevett's closet, maybe," Cathy suggested. "They've already looked in there for him, and if we could hide it high on a shelf, under something, they'd overlook it if they poked in there again."

So they boosted Ross up in Mr. Trevett's high-ceilinged closet. The boy had to reach, even with them holding him, and he was none too steady. But he finally got the things hidden under a row of leather hatboxes so they were not visible from the doorway.

Just then a bit of aged dust drifted down and made Patty sneeze. She let go of Ross to try to stop a second sneeze. He lost his balance, kicked Cathy accidentally, and made her lose her grip also, as he fell to the floor, banging his head against the back wall.

"Oh, Ross, I'm sorry! That dust—" Patty broke off her agitated whisper and shrank back, almost upsetting Cathy, as she stared at the wall that Ross's head had banged against. The wall had begun to move.

And as the three gasped in amazement and huddled back together, it swung open all the way.

"It's a d-door!" Patty gasped.

They peered into the darkness beyond. "A s-secret p-passage!" Ross stammered. "Let's see where it goes to!"

Patty gave a scared squeak and grabbed his sleeve to hold him back. "No! There's something there! It's moving!"

Cathy gasped, "It's coming this way!"

15   *The Great Escape!*

The white figure that was moving toward them out of the darkness of the narrow passageway was indistinct, but they could see that one arm was raised threateningly and there was some kind of cane or stick in its hand.

Patty gasped, "Jessie Belle!" And at that moment, she really believed in ghosts! "Let's get out of here!" she whispered urgently, pulling Cathy back into the bedroom.

But Cathy held firm. "Mr. Trevett!" she said, staring at the figure that had advanced into the light and was lowering a gold-headed cane.

It *was* Mr. Trevett—clad in a long, old-fashioned nightshirt, a knitted white nightcap with a long tassel, and a red and white striped burnous that he and his wife had picked up in Morocco many years before. He was a picturesque figure, to say the least.

Ross giggled and Patty nudged him reprovingly.

Mr. Trevett frowned at them. "Where did you three come from? And how did you find my secret door?"

"We found the fake ghost and the gold slipper—" Patty began.

"And we were hiding it on the shelf here for you, when Patty sneezed and I fell—and I knocked open the door—" Ross took it up.

"And Mrs. Burton and Byron are up in the gallery trying to find you so the men from Dr. Stanton's rest home can take you away on a stretcher—" Patty said it all in one breath.

"I thought that was the idea!" Mr. Trevett said with a scowl. "Well, they won't find me! Soon as I can get some clothes on, I'm going to go straight to the police—" He looked very fierce, his blue eyes snapping. "I'm going to tell them that miserable woman tried to feed me sleeping pills last night in my hot milk!"

"Oh!" Patty and Cathy exchanged knowing looks. And then Cathy asked anxiously, "How did you keep from taking them?"

The old gentleman chuckled. "Saw her dump some into the milk. Watched her in the mirror. Suspected that she might have a good reason for wanting me to sleep a long time. So when she left the milk for me to drink when I was ready for bed, I poured it down the sink. And when she sneaked back later, I pretended to be snoring."

"How did you keep from telling her off right then?" Patty asked indignantly. "I would have!"

He shook his head. "I had to see what she was up to. Besides, I hoped your father would drop in on his way to work and I could tell him about it. But he didn't."

"He had to go to the auto show. He won't be home till quite late," Cathy explained. "Special assignment."

"I was afraid something like that had happened. But I kept watching for him. And a few minutes ago, I saw those men with the stretcher arriving." He looked grim. "So I hid."

"Where does the secret passageway lead?" Ross asked excitedly.

"Between the walls, and comes out on the back stairs. I'd almost forgotten it, till I heard them coming up to get me. When I was a little tad, I used to raid the kitchen icebox at night, by way of that passage." He chuckled. "We'll sneak out that way as soon as I can get some clothes on."

"Somebody's coming!" Ross whispered suddenly.

The steps were close. Mr. Trevett pointed toward the closet, and a moment later, they had hastily ducked back into the closet after him. The door closed after them only a second before Mira and Byron came into the bedroom. It was a narrow escape.

"Quick! Straight ahead in the passage!" Trevett told them as he carefully closed the secret door at the back of the closet.

They were in complete darkness now, but with Patty in the lead, and moving as quietly as possible, the three went ahead while Mr. Trevett encouraged them from behind.

"That's it, youngsters," he whispered. "Keep going. We come out on the back stairs, just off the kitchen. We'll go through the kitchen and out to the garage. Hope I haven't forgotten how to drive that car! It's been some years since I tried it, but I guess I'll remember."

They found no one in the kitchen and reached the Duesenberg without mishap. They piled in, expecting at any minute that the men would see them from inside the house and come running out to stop them.

Mr. Trevett was fumbling with the starter key. "I've got it now," he said at last. "Away we go!" The motor roared, coughed, almost died, and then caught again and purred steadily. "Hold on!" He almost stripped the gears getting under way. The car roared down the driveway.

The two men from the rest home came running out of the house with Mira screeching after them, "Stop him! Stop him before he kills someone!" They dashed to their panel truck and drove wildly after the Duesenberg.

But by the time they reached the street, the Duesenberg was weaving through traffic two blocks away. They went after it. It was easy to see even at that distance. They soon started to overtake it.

Patty looked back. "They're gaining! Dash around this next corner and head for our house!" she told Mr. Trevett. "They can't touch you there!"

The old gentleman nodded his nightcapped head and swung around the corner on two wheels, but after he had straightened out the car he saw in the rearview mirror that the panel truck was less than a block behind him now. He didn't dare slow down for the Lane house. He had to keep going.

And then, suddenly, there was a parade going past at the next corner. He would have to stop, and the men would get him. He started to use his brake.

"No use, girls. We can't get through here," he said resignedly.

"But we can!" Patty yelled excitedly. "It's the horseless carriage club and we can make believe we're an entry! They can't follow us!"

Mr. Trevett took a quick glance behind him.

The white panel truck was stymied for a moment behind a limousine.

"We'll try!" he agreed hastily, and honked imperiously for the spectators to get out of his way. After a glance, they did. And Mr. Trevett wheeled the big car into line in front of a handsome red Mercedes-Benz Supercharged Cabriolet '37, which practically had to stand on its nose to keep from climbing onto the rear of the intruding Duesenberg.

The face that looked out at them from the Mercedes' driver's compartment was that of Martin Lane's publisher, J. R. Castle, and to say that he was annoyed was putting it mildly.

A moment later, when he had recognized the two Lane girls, now perched on the rear seat and waving to the crowds, he was positively apoplectic.

And not long afterward, Patty was sure he was almost ready to fire his managing editor— when the Duesenberg won first prize and his own car only second.

But after he had found out what had happened

and that Martin had had nothing to do with it all, he generously forgave everyone concerned and had himself photographed with his arm over Mr. Trevett's burnous-clad figure, while Patty on one side and Cathy on the other smilingly showed off the silver trophies the two cars had won.

Cathy was still uneasy about what had become of the two men in white jackets, but she need not have been, she learned later. They had tried to get past into the line of old cars and continue the chase, but they had been barred by annoyed spectators. So they had given up without much of a struggle. After all, they were only employees at the rest home. It would be up to Dr. Stanton what to do next.

But Dr. Stanton had been watching a television coverage of the car show, and it had convinced him that it might be just as well to forget Mrs. Burton's charges against her uncle. After all, the old fellow might be an eccentric—many elderly people were—but he seemed to have some powerful friends. And Mrs. Burton was obviously a hysterical type herself. So he instructed his secretary that he would be "out" when the lady called again.

But Mira did not call. She had seen the television show, too. Byron had called excitedly to her from his room to come and look at it. They had watched it to the bitter end. They had seen Council President Peterson beaming his congratulations toward Mr. Owen Trevett, the winner. And they had heard him describe Mr. Trevett as a "public-spirited citizen who has so generously offered his magnificent historical relic of a mansion on Brooklyn Heights to our city for a paltry sum, to prevent its destruction by heartless money-grubbers." He had somewhat coyly added that the city council might soon have some happy news about that to convey to the citizens after its next and final meeting for the summer.

As the happy scene had faded out on a close-up of Mr. Trevett modestly bowing to heavy applause, Byron had risen with a yawn. "Well, we tried! I still don't know where we slipped up. Better start packing our bags."

And Mira agreed grimly. "I can't help feeling

that that Patty Lane and her cousin Cathy are to blame somehow. I knew the moment I laid eyes on them that they were troublemakers!"

But there were quite a few other people who wouldn't have agreed with that verdict. Natalie and Martin, for instance. And Owen Trevett. Even Ross, who was rather proud of them both.

It was a happy group that gathered at the Lane dinner table a few hours later. Happy because it now seemed certain that before long Mr. Trevett would have his heart's wish to go back to Scotland to live. They would all be sorry to see him go, of course, but they would keep in touch with him. He would always have a home to come to at their place if he wanted it. He promised to write regularly, and he had hinted to Patty that there were other pretty baubles like the necklace in his safe and she could expect to receive one of them for her help.

Even that exciting news couldn't quite bring Patty's usual broad smile to her face. She was trying hard to be gay, but it was difficult with one ear cocked toward the telephone.

They had almost finished dinner when the doorbell rang. Martin sent her to see who was there, and Patty went with dragging feet, complaining under her breath about always having to answer the door.

She was a long time coming back. Ross had already laid claim to her dessert when she came in—with Richard in tow. They were both beaming happily. Richard had a smudge of lipstick on one cheek, and Patty was boldly wearing her ID bracelet on the sleeve of her cashmere sweater.

They made a place for Richard at the table, and everyone was very gay, especially Patty, whose smile was beamed at all present, even Ross, who was slightly stunned by it.

And Cathy hoped that Patty wouldn't suspect that she had phoned Richard and scolded him into acting sensibly and forgetting all about being jealous of Byron.

She was glad he had taken her advice. Now all was peaceful again. Well, at least for the time being! Until some other dashing young man came along to catch her favorite cousin's eye!

Whitman ADVENTURE and MYSTERY Books

Adventure Stories for GIRLS and BOYS ...

TIMBER TRAIL RIDERS
The Long Trail North
The Texas Tenderfoot
The Luck of Black Diamond
Mystery of the Hollywood Horse
The Mysterious Dude

POWER BOYS SERIES
The Haunted Skyscraper
The Flying Skeleton

DONNA PARKER
In Hollywood
At Cherrydale
Special Agent
On Her Own
A Spring to Remember
Mystery at Arawak
Takes a Giant Step

TROY NESBIT SERIES
Sand Dune Pony
Diamond Cave Mystery
Indian Mummy Mystery
Mystery at Rustlers' Fort

New Stories About Your Television Favorites ...

Dr. Kildare
Assigned to Trouble
The Magic Key

Janet Lennon at Camp Calamity

Walt Disney's Annette
Mystery at Smugglers' Cove
Desert Inn Mystery
Sierra Summer
Mystery at Moonstone Bay
Mystery at Medicine Wheel

Combat! The Counterattack

The Beverly Hillbillies

Lassie
Secret of the Summer
Forbidden Valley
Mystery at Blackberry Bog

Lucy and the Madcap Mystery

Patty Duke and Mystery Mansion